GETTING THROUGH

TALES of CORONA and COMMUNITY

D1714923

Edited by Gerald Elias
April, 2020

Dedicated to all those on the front lines—
From the hospital workers and the first responders,
To the teachers and the parents,
To the truckers and the supermarket cashiers.

Getting Through: Tales of Corona and Community

Table of Contents

Introduction

You try to keep busy. You try to stay positive. But after a period of extended confinement, on any level, it's easy to become bored and dispirited. No restaurants, no shopping, no sporting events. No work! What to do?

I consider myself lucky. My cupboard is well-stocked and I'm comfortable with a lot of alone time. Writing. Practicing the violin. Watching the news on PBS, mysteries on Netflix. Cooking. I've been doing all those things for years. I try to avoid too much thumb twiddling.

I was working on Cloudy With a Chance of Murder, the next book in my Daniel Jacobus mystery series, thinking about how writing keeps me engaged. Kept my mind off the 24-7 coronavirus news cycle and off of strategies to shop at the supermarket without dying. The writing kept me positive.

Light bulb! That's when the idea occurred to me to try to encourage others to become similarly occupied. But how? In addition to my traditionally published mysteries, I've published a bunch of things independently and have developed a bit of facility getting books up and running. *So, how about a short story anthology?* I thought. Let anyone and everyone become a published author. Within our individual isolation, create a community. Getting Through: Tales of Corona and Community was born.

Subject matter: anything, basically. As long as it's somehow at least tangentially connected to the pandemic. And if it isn't, that's okay, too. Fiction, nonfiction, poetry, dystopian, essay, memoir, humor, science fiction, children's stories. Stories of faith and of hope. Stories of biting satire and of empathy. Love letters from parents to children. It's all good. People are creative in many ways.

Speed was important. I wanted it to be released quickly so that all those who are still confined have something entertaining to keep them distracted. But with so much creativity being churned out on the internet on a daily basis, who would read it? Who would buy it?

Next idea: Send all the profits to a charity that everyone would consider worthwhile, and whose good works will be sorely needed in the months to come. It didn't take long to think of that one. The American Red Cross.

So that's it in a nutshell. Within days I received two dozen stories—some from old friends, many from new friends whose faces I've never seen; from amateur writers to established authors; from every corner of the US and from England and Italy; from scientists, musicians, birders, high school students...you name it. Some pieces are deadly serious, others a touch bizarre, and some I hope will give you a chuckle in these difficult times.

Thank you, writers, for stepping up to the plate. Thank you, readers for becoming part of our new, expanding community. And we need not stop here. If you'd like to send me *your* story, or your artwork, or your cartoon, don't hesitate. If we get enough, maybe we could do a second volume. So please pass the word, and if you spread the goodwill faster than this damn virus, we'll have a bestseller in no time!

Gerald Elias, Editor
April, 2020.

Cello Reverie During COVID-19
by Anonymous

I have had asthma since elementary school, so it's essential I take every precaution to protect my health during these extraordinary times. That's why I was driving to the grocery store at 5:00 a.m. on a freezing Saturday morning. The neighborhood was dark and still; no people, no moving cars. Just me.

Due to the coronavirus epidemic, everyone was staying in their homes. Because the "Rule of 10" was in force, meaning only ten people or fewer could be in a group, the supermarket opened early, serving individual customers only after the store had been sanitized and freshly stocked. There would be toilet paper on the shelves!

But asthma was not what was on my mind as I drove. On this cold morning, my mind was filled with the warmth of the nineteenth century Czech composer, Antonin Dvorak, his stunning cello concerto, and two virtuoso cellists.

For the last five years, I've written program notes for our local symphony orchestra. Next year one of the scheduled works is the Dvorak cello concerto. In researching my program notes, I read biographies of two unparalleled cellists, Janos Starker and Mstislav Rostropovich.

Janos Starker, acclaimed for his fabulous technique and lyrical playing, and as a renowned pedagogue, was born in Budapest, Hungary, in 1924. His early music education took place in the chaos of air raids and bombings in Hungary during World War II, terrifying times for the young cellist. Starker ultimately escaped to Romania, and finally Austria. After coming to America, he served as principal cellist for the Metropolitan Opera Orchestra and the Chicago Symphony Orchestra. He then went on to become Professor of Cello at Indiana University, "Home of the Hoosiers"!

Mstislav Rostropovich was born in Baku, Russia, in 1927. His parents were musicians and his first cello teacher was his father. He later studied at the Moscow Conservatory while over twenty-million citizens of the Soviet Union were being killed in World War II. Though Rostropovich contemplated going to Leningrad to study, that city was strangled under Nazi Germany's siege. In 1974, after he was forced to leave Russia, his fame spread worldwide, and he later became music director of the National Symphony Orchestra in Washington D.C. Rostropovich died in 2007.

I had been feeling sorry for myself having to endure the hardships due to COVID-19—stay indoors, no gathering at a local cafe with friends, no March Madness. But thinking about these two cellists made me realize how my experience pales in comparison to the extreme deprivation they endured in their younger days, though their cruel conditions were caused by the outbreak of a war, not an outbreak of a pandemic.

I entered the grocery store parking lot. Five cars were there. I shivered as I walked to the market doors. Grabbing a shopping cart, I could smell the store's cleanliness. This put my mind at ease. Following my list, I automatically picked out the necessities. While I shopped, I sang to myself, recalling performances of these two supreme musicians.

As a college music major, I was fortunate enough to get a part-time office job—a paying job—with a "top ten" orchestra. Closeness to the administration and musicians occasionally allowed me to sneak in and listen to a portion of a rehearsal. One week, Starker was playing the Dvorak concerto with the orchestra! I sat in the back of the seats for all the rehearsals. I smiled at the memory, and it warmed me up a little.

As I continued my solitary shopping, my smile broadened, recalling a particular performance by Mstislav Rostropovich of a solo recital in the big orchestra hall for a fundraiser. Oh, how exciting! As a poor college student, I didn't expect to attend because the tickets were so expensive. But then, a member of the orchestra management, who knew I played piano, asked if I would turn pages for the cellist's accompanist! Of course

I was eager to help out! The recital was memorable!! And Mr. Rostropovich even gave me a little peck on the cheek, I guess for not missing a single page turn!

But that wasn't the end. Several years later I was teaching music in another city that had a "Big Five" orchestra. The Dvorak Cello Concerto was on the program in preparation for a European tour. Rostropovich was the guest artist. Such a gorgeous concerto. No one plays it like he did.

One condition of being in the sanitized grocery store was having to bag the groceries myself. I didn't mind, because as I bagged I continued "listening" to the Dvorak Concerto for Violoncello and Orchestra uninterrupted.

The drive home was happy and one of relief. I had enough groceries for two months. But as I drove, I also thought about how Janos Starker and Mstislav Rostropovich were able to transcend the most trying times by making beautiful music. I just knew I would make it through COVID-19 if I cared for myself as much as they cared for their art!

Dvorak. Starker. Rostropovich.

Inspiration.

The author holds an undergraduate degree in music and graduate degree in business administration.

Boots on the Ground
by Robert Baldwin

Oh, to put boots on the ground—
uneven terrain, with rocks and roots
and streams to ford. Unpaved *terra firma,*
a physicality—a connection from
breath to breath and dust to dust.

      This temporary ban
      but a pause, yet
      viscerally binding.

The irregular light dazzles there;
sunlight versus shadow, a seasonal ebb-flow,
a coming and a going; a canyon's cycle,
through another seasonal turn.
I recognize it in rocks and gravel,
witness it in plants and animals,
honor it with both inhalation and expiration,
from single molecule to entire mountainside.
Expressed in both boulder and sand—timeless,
yet also found in the mayfly—alive mere hours.

      Somewhere in-between lies us,
      you and me—closer to the fly than the stone,
      perhaps—and we too are part of the story worth telling;
      not of empires or kings,
      but of suns, galaxies, universes.

Lacking such sage-hood, I nonetheless
take notice, sensing something

greater than myself.

> So I lace and place boots
> on the ground, again feeling
> the nativity of the Earth surging
> though my veins and traveling,
> from sole to spirit.

Robert Baldwin, an orchestra conductor and professor at the University of Utah School of Music, has had his works published in recent issues of Utah Life, Grey Sparrow Journal, Haiku Journal and Poetry Quarterly.

Lettere ai Nostri Figli
di Riccardo Betti e Johanna Fridrich (Italia)

Di padre in figlia

Cara Leandra,

Scrivo questa lettera con il forte desiderio di aiutare te e le persone che avrai scelto di avere intorno a te quando la leggerai per darti il ricordo più vivo e vero di questa strana primavera.

Si perché mentre per te questi giorni sono belli e ancor più pieni del solito, intorno alla nostra "casotta" il mondo sta, prima ancora che cambiando, soffrendo molto.

Spero che negli anni che verranno e per merito dei quali sarai diventata una donna io e tua madre saremmo stati in grado di mantenere gli obiettivi che ci eravamo posti: che tu sia forte, serena e libera, capace così da trovare in ogni avversità una nuova strada.

Un tizio un po' stravagante che nei libri avrai visto in fotografie in bianco e nero con dei capelli un po' arruffati ed i baffoni nel 1929 capii che "*non possiamo pretendere che le cose cambino, se continuiamo a fare le stesse cose. La crisi è la più grande benedizione per le persone e le nazioni, perché la crisi porta progressi. La creatività nasce dall'angoscia come il giorno nasce dalla notte scura. E' nella crisi che sorge l'inventiva, le scoperte e le grandi strategie. Chi supera la crisi supera se stesso senza essere superato.*"

Einstein lo scriveva in riferimento alla grande crisi economica del 1929. Io spero che queste parole abbiamo, dal 2020 in poi, fatto parte del tuo modo di affrontare la vita.

Si perché mentre abbiamo avuto la fortuna di trovarci in questo preciso momento storico in un'oasi, in una piccola valle del cuore verde d'Italia, l'Umbria, dove il virus "Covid-19" (o come lo chiami tu in questi giorni "coronavirus quel cattivo") terrorizza, ma più per quanto vediamo e sentiamo che per quanto percepiamo con i nostri sensi, il nostro Paese sta affrontando una delle emergenze più gravi dalla nascita della Repubblica.

I tuoi nonni come me, come tua madre, non avevamo mai vissuto tutto questo.

Non c'era mai capitato di avere la necessità di essere così attenti alle conferenze stampa dei nostri governanti, di commuoverci all'appello dei medici e degli infermieri che ci chiedevano di stare a casa, di chiudere tutto perché dovevamo arrestare la diffusione di un'influenza che abbiamo capito a nostre spese essere letale.

Non c'era mai capitato di avere limitazioni, di buon senso prima che per ordine, alla nostra libertà, con le richieste di spostarsi il meno possibile e soltanto per motivi di necessità, come fare la spesa non più di una volta a settimana o acquistare farmaci.

Non c'era mai capitato di fare attenzione alla "distanza sociale", di evitare di stringere la mano e, con gli amici, darsi un fraterno abbraccio.

Non c'era mai capitato di vedere chiudere il tuo asilo e ogni altra scuola del Paese fino ad un tempo sconosciuto, né vedere chiusi bar e negozi.

Anche se non te ne sei accorta, mentre avevi la possibilità di raccogliere fiori in giardino, di giocare vicino al tuo laghetto preferito, di fare maschere da unicorno e vedere, ogni tanto, qualche cartone animato in più del solito, tutto questo accadeva.

Accadeva che tuo papà si commuoveva ad ascoltare il nostro Presidente della Repubblica o ad ascoltare gli interventi di alcuni parlamentari che venivano dalle zone delle regioni più martoriate, si preoccupava nel sentire e leggere notizie di ciò che stava accadendo soltanto a poche centinaia di chilometri dalla nostra serenità.

In quei giorni, di tanto in tanto io e tua madre ricordiamo anche il tempo in cui, neanche tanti anni fa a dire il vero, ci siamo re-incontrati e abbiamo sentito forte l'amore di viverci.

Parte di quell'amore deriva proprio dalla capacità di credere che andrà tutto bene indipendentemente da come andrà, e questo per il semplice motivo che è nei nostri caratteri l'ideale forte di potersi adattare ad ogni cambiamento.

Figlia mia, spero che anche tu come noi, abbia salde radici su cui poggiarti, ma rami in grado di affrontare ogni nuova sfida con la viva intelligenza di trovare opportunità e soluzioni laddove, purtroppo, pare più facile aspettare.

Questo affinché tu ricordi come quei giorni non furono finzione per darti serenità o per non fare preoccupare una bimba di neanche 5 anni.

Iniziai a lavorare da casa per ridurre i contatti con le persone ma di giorno in giorno tornai ad apprezzare la libertà di vedere te e tuo fratello ad ogni pausa.

E così abbiamo avuto di nuovo giorni pieni insieme, a cucinare, a leggere libri o a vedere cartoni animati. Tornammo a fare i giochi che avevamo inventato insieme un po' di mesi prima che nascesse il tuo fratellino.

Con l'occasione insegnai a tuoi nonni (che devo dire con mio stupore impararono velocemente) ad utilizzare *Skype* per poterti vedere e per poter parlare un po' con te visto quanto gli mancavi.

Abitavano vicino alla nostra cosa, qualche chilometro di distanza, ma non potevamo andare da loro.

Facevamo progetti su cosa avremmo fatto una volta tornati alla "normalità" anche se, ammetto, su questo non fui sincero fino in fondo con te.

Perché in cuor mio speravo che, riaperti i negozi, le aziende, con le persone lontane delle terapie intensive, in un tempo in cui non ci sarebbero state più conferenze stampa alle 18 e messaggi di sostegno alla popolazione, alcune cose di questo tempo ce le saremmo ricordate.

Segui la tua strada Leandra, e fallo in ogni parte del mondo in cui questa ti condurrà, ma fallo con la giusta attenzione alla natura, avendo cura in ogni fase della tua vita di conoscerti e di vivere in armonia con te stessa e con ciò che ti circonda.

Solo così, credo, altre distanze sociali, quarantene o sciagure varie – più semplicemente, come li chiamo io, *cambiamenti* – troveranno in te il primo nemico da affrontare.

In questa occasione siamo stati fortunati ad essere dove siamo, ma non è detto che questa fortuna possa ripetersi o che possa ripetersi sempre.

C'è dunque qualcosa da imparare anche in una posizione di fortuna come la nostra. Ma cosa? Non so quali articoli di giornale o video messaggi potrai reperire nel tuo tempo ma oggi, a emergenza ancora in atto, con alle spalle la giornata di ieri nella quale il nostro Paese a raggiunto il numero più alto di morti nelle 24 ore (quasi mille) posso darti di aver imparato che nessun luogo di questo pianeta è davvero così lontano rispetto ad un altro; che ognuno può fare qualcosa ma nessuno può fare tutto (io, per esempio, sono un avvocato e non posso diventare un virologo seguendo interviste o guardando serie tv), che la paura aiuta a sbagliare e che il conoscersi ed il sentirsi in armonia con se stessi rappresenta a mio avviso la più grande forza a nostra disposizione.

C'è poi quello che si può imparare, anzi che si deve imparare in ogni situazione; io, ad esempio, da Covid-19 ho imparato ad avere rispetto della natura, che nelle sue infinite forme ci ricorda che non siamo noi i padroni della terra e che la vita c'è stata donata, che saper cucire e cucinare non è affatto *demodè* e che, per quanto ad oggi connessione e *web* possano annullare le distanze fisiche, è sempre meglio avere una montagna di libri ad attenderci in salotto o in camera da letto.

Compito mio, da genitore, è far di tutto affinché questo possa avvenire, che tu sia pronta non ad un nuovo virus ma alla vita di cui questo virus o un giorno un altro potrà far parte; compito tuo Leandra invece è, da figlia, da individuo, da cittadina, quello di farti trovare pronta, con la giusta positività e serenità, ad affrontare ogni momento, bello, difficile o spaventoso che sia.

Con l'amore di un papà,

r.

Di madre in figlio

Amore mio.

Che dormi rannicchiato contro il mio fianco, nell'incavo del braccio con la boccuccia aperta e il respiro regolare...all'improvviso uno strillino nel sonno perché ti stanno spuntando i primi dentini...

Un anno fa eri ancora nella mia pancia. eri un pensiero, un'idea che scalciava nuotando...

La luce della luna filtra dalla finestra del tetto. In questo momento il mondo sembra fermo, silenzioso e sereno come te e invece sta cambiando, sta cambiando tutto...

Forse la vita come l'ho conosciuta io da quando sono nata tra pochi mesi non esisterà più...Viviamo, noi grandi, questa strana sensazione di essere parte di quello che sarà Storia...Mi sono chiesta spesso come accadono davvero gli eventi...i cambiamenti epocali...posto che non c'è un interruttore che fa clic, davvero tutto scorre placido come sempre solo che il fiume cambia impercettibilmente il suo percorso...Cambia letto quasi di nascosto...?Quando si prendono sul serio le cose? Quando ci si rassegna? Quando si scappa? Quando si decide di combattere? Le donne iraniane prima del '79 credevano davvero che sarebbe successo quello che poi è successo? O gli ebrei europei degli anni 30? Siamo noi adesso le rane nell'acqua calda che non si accorgono di come i gradi salgano pericolosamente?

Oppure tutto passerà improvvisamente come è cominciato e torneremo alla vita di prima? Dopo 1mesi sospesi nella storia ci sveglieremo come da un sogno?

Mia nonna è nata negli anni 10 del 900, in una Parigi illuminata dai lampioni e percorsa da carrozze ed è morta nei primi anni del 2000, in un nuovo millennio, un mondo di telefoni senza fili, minigonne e internet, l'uomo era stato sulla luna e un concorde ci metteva 3 ore e mezza a volare da Londra a New York!

Ma in realtà anche io, che sono nata nel 1984 ho visto il mondo cambiare vorticosamente. Sono nata in una Germania ancora divisa in due, sono cresciuta con cabine telefoniche e appuntamenti da rispettare con meticolosità, a scuola le ricerche si facevano sulle enciclopedie, i viaggi in aereo erano ancora un lusso e i videogiochi non realtà virtuali ma piccoli schermi in bianco e nero...Ora che sono madre, tua e di Leandra, vivo in questo nuovo mondo ad alta velocità, sempre connessi e raggiungibili, con qualunque informazione a disposizione in qualsiasi momento...Ma non ricordo davvero come è successo...Forse è vero che al progresso ci si abitua velocemente. Ho fatto le superiori senza smartphone e Wikipedia, avevo quasi 20 anni quando ho avuto la prima macchina fotografica digitale, ho scritto la tesi prima di Facebook...Ho viaggiato senza Google maps...La mia prima macchina non aveva neanche il servosterzo figuriamoci il Tomtom! Ma ora tutto questo anche a me sembra scontato, normale, dovuto. E davvero credevo che tu avresti potuto avere un giorno a disposizione una tecnologia che a me sembra fantascienza...robot, teletrasporto, macchine volanti, crociere nello spazio...Ma quanto veloci si può andare davvero?

Sotto questa luna sempre uguale, con il tuo respiro nelle orecchie, la notte è ferma e immobile. Ma in questo stesso momento negli ospedali di tutto il mondo c'è frastuono, c'è frenesia, luce, velocità, rumore, stanchezza, paura, adrenalina...C'è eroismo e c'è solitudine...C'è rabbia, avidità, fretta e morte.

E' come ritrovarsi catapultati in un romanzo...La vita che cambia nel giro di pochi giorni. A febbraio abbiamo festeggiato il mio compleanno con un picnic improvvisato al parco, ricordi? Il tuo papà è andato a prendere la pizza, c'erano i miei genitori, Leandra che giocava sull' altalena, tu che avevi appena imparato a stare seduto da solo...E intorno c'era gente di tutti i tipi, gente che chiacchierava, che correva, che portava i cani a passeggio...Si sapeva già della Cina, ma così come si sente di un terremoto, un'eruzione vulcanica, un'alluvione dall' altra parte del mondo...Lo senti, ti dispiace, magari fai un bonifico o un sms di beneficenza ne parli con qualcuno, condividi un post sui social e poi, te lo scordi. Le informazioni seppur presenti scivolano in sottofondo...Il sottofondo della tua vita che continua come prima...In genere di corsa e non ti fa soffermare, riflettere, provare empatia...Sul giornale la stessa notizia scivola dalla prima pagina a quelle interne e poi in genere scompare...E le tue giornate continuano...

Questa volta invece dopo essere scivolata in fondo la notizia è esplosa di nuovo sulle prime pagine, dalla Cina ora la malattia era arrivata qui, in Italia, via aereo. Nascosto tra le valige dei turisti e le ventiquattrore degli uomini d'affari, passato di mano in mano con i soldi di una mancia e l'abbraccio di un bambino.

Il mondo da grande che è appare ora sempre più piccolo...i confini meno politici e più naturali, quindi, in realtà è come se non ci fossero... Niente trattiene l'aria, niente trattiene questa subdola malattia...Forse ancora più subdola perché non sembra così spaventosa...

La gente non prendeva sul serio la cosa. Sembrava un' influenza... nessuno voleva limitarsi, cambiare...

In un attimo invece tutto è cambiato...Sembrava di leggere Orwell...

Le informazioni si rincorrono, gli scienziati si attaccano a vicenda, vengono date e poi smentite notizie. Prima tutti dovevamo restare calmi e andare avanti, poi all'improvviso tutto doveva fermarsi. Dobbiamo nasconderci dal virus, dobbiamo proteggere chi è meno forte, anziani, malati, immunodepressi...chiuderci nelle nostre case perché gli ospedali stanno collassando...

Siamo 60 milioni di abitanti, come si possono fermare tutti? Come si può fermare una malattia così veloce? Sembrava impossibile, invece nel giro di pochi giorni hanno chiuso scuole, cinema, librerie, biblioteche, bar, ristoranti, poi anche negozi e parte delle fabbriche...Insomma quasi tutto...Le strade sono vuote, non è permesso uscire se non per comprare da mangiare o andare a lavorare (per quei pochi che ancora possono)... Non sembra vero...E la cosa strana è che non si sa fino a quando e non si sa cosa succederà...Sopravvivrà la nostra economia? Sopravvivrà il concetto di Europa unita? Torneremo a viaggiare liberi come prima? Ad abbracciare sconosciuti? Quanti strascichi porteremo di queste settimane? Anche psicologici?

A volte mi spaventano le persone...L'opinione pubblica manovrata, manipolata. La rabbia che nasce da questa sensazione di impotenza e trasforma gli animi...I vicini che denunciano dalle loro finestre se vedono qualcuno correre solo per il parco o uscire più di una volta con il cane, i genitori esasperati dai figli, le regole sociali, ma anche le libertà personali pericolosamente messe in discussione...

Noi siamo così fortunati...Sembra ancora una lunga vacanza...Papà lavora da casa e improvvisamente invece di 12 ore al giorno ne lavora 6 e ha tanto più tempo per stare con noi...Abbiamo una casa grande o un immenso giardino, c'è anche il bosco...La primavera esplode tra i rami e srotola tappeti di margherite...Con Leandra facciamo maschere di carta, biscotti di pasta e sale, marmellate, disegni...prepariamo pane pizza e pasta fatta in casa...

A tua sorella già mancano gli amici dell' asilo, i nonni, la danza, le lezioni di violino...Spero che l' isolamento finisca prima che lei se ne renda davvero conto. Ho paura di vedere un giorno il suo viso intristirsi, di vederla sentirsi in gabbia, di non "bastarle"...

Tu sei ancora così piccolo, il mondo che verrà, qualunque cosa sarà, sarà il "tuo" mondo, non avrai ricordi del prima...Eppure non so immaginare come potrebbe essere se tutto questo continuasse e tu crescessi qui, tra queste mura solo con noi, senza altri visi, altri stimoli, altri bambini.

Vorrei riuscire a vivere oltre l'angoscia...riuscire a vedere le opportunità di tutto questo...più che vederle, realizzarle. Dare un contributo al mondo che sarà. Lo so, e' facile avere il cuore pieno di speranza e gratitudine se hai accanto la tua famiglia, una casa con giardino che ti permette di respirare la primavera, un marito che anche se diversamente per adesso continua a lavorare, un orto dove coltivare

14

verdure, una libreria piena di libri, una cucina piena di cibo...Ma questa è la mia vita, ed è sul piatto. Che sia un'offerta votiva o la posta in un gioco d'azzardo non so...So che la proteggerò, ma che cercherò anche di alleggerirla, di mantenerne l' essenza non il superfluo, di condividere...Ho viaggiato e vissuto in varie parti del mondo...Ho amici e famigliari che hanno fatto come me, i miei affetti sono sparsi nei continenti, non so quando li rivedrò, se le distanze torneranno ad essere grandi come un secolo fa, ma va bene così, anche rinunciando a tanto di quello che oggi ho e che mi sembra indispensabile, so che dalla crisi nasce il cambiamento, necessario, essenziale, anche positivo, ma che senza crisi non avemmo accettato di intraprendere o avuto tempo di vedere.

Ti guardo in penumbra...annuso il tuo odore...ringrazio il cielo che tu non sia più nella mia pancia...

Avrei avuto tanta paura a partorire adesso...e invece ho il privilegio di poter rinascere con te, affacciarmi a questo nuovo mondo come stai facendo tu...seguire i tuoi sguardi curiosi, le tue risate di entusiasmo, il coraggio e la deliziosa incoscienza di oltrepassare i limiti...Per te che ogni giorno è ancora il primo e porta con sé visioni profumi ed esperienze nuove, nuovissime...Imparare da te che non hai nulla da perdere, ma solo da esplorare, scoprire, accogliere e vivere! Nella nascita c'è la chiave della Natura che non si ferma...la prepotenza della vita che se ne infischia delle sovrastrutture...La gioia che vince la paura. Con ogni respiro mi insegni qualcosa ed è bello, spento il baccano, sentirti distintamente... Bello avere tempo. Tempo per abbracciare tuo papà e sentire in ogni fibra del corpo che lo amo e che insieme siamo giunco, che possiamo piegarci ma non ci spezzeremo, possiamo mettere in discussione tutto perché l'essenziale è qui tra le nostre braccia e siete voi, Orlando e Leandra. Tutto andrà bene perché siamo insieme e in un modo o l'altro lo affronteremo...

Riccardo Betti e Johanna Fridrich, sposati dal 2014, genitori di due bambini, Leandra di 4 anni e mezzo o Orlando di 10 mesi. Riccardo è avvocato, Johanna tre le tante cose ha fatto per anni la pasticcera. Lui italiano, lei papà francese e mamma tedesca ma vissuta in Italia fin da piccola. La loro casa è in Umbria, in mezzo al verde, vicino alle loro famiglie e insieme a Iago, un bel labrador nero con il muso imbiancato.

Letters to Our Children

by Riccardo Betti & Johanna Fridrich (Italy)

Translation assistance by Sergio Pallottelli

Father to daughter

Dear Leandra,

I write this letter to you because I feel it's so important for you and for those you will choose to be part of your life to have the most vivid and true memory of this strange spring.

Yes, because while for you these days are beautiful and even more fulfilling than usual, the world is suffering, even more than it is changing, around our little cottage.

I hope that in the years to come, when you have become a woman, everything your mother and I hoped for you will come true: that you may be strong, serene and free, capable of overcoming any adversity you might encounter.

In 1929, a mildly eccentric fellow with disheveled hair and mustache, whose black-and-white photos you've seen in books, understood that we cannot expect things to change "if we keep doing the same things." He said, "A crisis can be a real blessing to any person, to any nation. For all crises bring progress. Creativity is born from anguish, just like the day is born from the dark night. It's in crisis that inventiveness is born, as well as discoveries made and big strategies. He who overcomes crisis, overcomes himself, without getting overcome."

Einstein wrote that in reference to the great economic crisis of 1929, but I hope that these words will, from 2020 onwards, be part of your way of facing life.

Yes, because while we were lucky enough in this precise historical moment to find ourselves in an oasis, in our little valley in the green heart of Italy—Umbria—where the COVID-19 virus—or as it is called these days, "Coronavirus that villain"—terrified us more because of what we saw and heard about it than from what we actually experienced, our country faced one of the most serious emergencies since the birth of the Republic.

Your grandparents, like me and like your mother, had never experienced any of this.

There had never been the need to be so attentive to government press conferences, to be moved by doctors and nurses who appealed to us to stay at home, to close everything because we had to stop the spread of a virus that we understood to be lethal.

There had never been a need to restrict our freedom other than by common sense. But then the law ordered us to go outside as infrequently as possible and only for reasons of necessity, such as shopping no more than once a week, or to buy medicine.

There had never been a need to pay attention to "social distancing," to avoid shaking hands and, with friends, to give each other a warm embrace.

There had never been a need for your kindergarten or any other school in the country to be closed until further notice, nor to see cafés and shops shut down.

Even though you didn't notice, while you had the opportunity to pick flowers in the garden, to play near your favorite pond, to make unicorn masks, and to watch, occasionally, more cartoons than usual, all this happened.

It happened that your dad, listening to our President of the Republic or to speeches of senators from the most tormented regions, was emotionally moved to hear and read news of what was happening only a few hundred kilometers from our serenity.

There will be a time in the future when your mother and I will reminisce about these days as a time when we met again and we felt the love of living here.

Part of that love derives from the conviction to believe that everything will eventually be fine, regardless of how things seem at the moment. Simply, the strong ideal of being able to adapt to any change is in our characters.

My daughter, I hope that you too, like us, will have firm roots on which to rest and with branches capable of reaching out to every new challenge with the lively intelligence of finding opportunities and solutions, where waiting, though it might seem easier, would be the less fortunate path.

This is so that you remember how these days really were, not so much as a way to give you peace of mind or even as a way to not make a little five-year-old girl worry.

As I started working more from home in order to reduce contact with people, day after day as I returned I cherished the freedom to see you and your brother at every possible moment.

And so we had full days together again: cooking, reading books or watching cartoons. We went back to playing the games we had invented together a few months before your little brother was born.

I took the opportunity to teach your grandparents (which I must say to my amazement they quickly learned) to use Skype, so that they would be able to see you and to be able to talk a little with you, given how much they missed you. Even though they lived near our home, only a few kilometers away, we couldn't go to them.

We made plans about what we would do once we got back to "normal" even though, I admit, I wasn't completely honest with you about this. Because in my heart I hoped that, once shops and companies reopened and there were no more people in intensive care, in a time when there would be no more press conferences at six p.m. and messages of support to the population, some things of this time would continue.

Follow your path, Leandra, wherever in the world it will lead you, but do it with the right attention to nature, taking care in every phase of your life to know yourself and to live in harmony with yourself and with what surrounds you.

Only in this way, I believe, future social distancing, quarantines or various disasters—more simply, as I call them, changes—will find you to be a strong adversary. On this occasion we were lucky to be where we were, but there is no guarantee this luck can repeat itself. There is therefore something to learn even in our lucky position. But what?

I don't know what newspaper articles or video messages you will be able to find in your time; but today, with the emergency still in progress, with yesterday behind us, in which our country reached the highest number of deaths in twenty-four hours (almost a thousand) I can tell you that I have learned that no place on this planet is really that far from another; that everyone can do something but nobody can do everything (for example, I am a lawyer and I cannot become a virologist following interviews or watching TV series); that fear contributes to making mistakes; and that knowing and feeling in harmony with oneself represents, in my opinion, the greatest strength at our disposal.

Then there is what you can learn, or rather what you must learn in any situation. I, for example, learned from COVID-19 to have respect for nature, which in its infinite forms reminds us that we are not the masters of the earth, and that life has been given to us; that knowing how to sew and cook is not at all out-of-fashion; and that although today internet connection and the web can eliminate physical distances, it is always better to have a mountain of books waiting for us in the living room or bedroom.

My task, as a parent, is to do everything possible for this to happen, that you are ready not necessarily for a new virus but for a life which may present similar challenges. Your task Leandra, as a daughter, as an individual, as a citizen, is to find yourself ready, with positivity and serenity, to face every moment, as beautiful, difficult, or frightening that it may be.

With the love of a dad,

R.

Mother to son

My love...

You sleep curled up against my side, in the hollow of my arm with your little mouth open and regular breathing...suddenly a tiny shriek in your sleep because the first teeth are popping up...

A year ago you were still in my belly...you were a thought, an idea, that kicked while swimming...

The moonlight filters through the roof window...At this moment the world seems still, silent and peaceful like you, but instead it is changing, everything is changing...

Maybe life as I have known it since I was born, in a few months will no longer exist...We adults live with this strange feeling of being part of what will be History...I often wondered how events really happen...the epochal changes...given that there is not a switch that clicks, really, everything flows placidly as always, only that the river changes its path imperceptibly...changes its bed almost secretly...? When do we take things seriously? When do we give up? When do we run away? When do we decide to fight? Did Iranian women before '79 really believe that what happened next would happen? Or the European Jews of the 1930s? Are we now the frogs in hot water, who do not notice how dangerously the temperature rises?

Or will everything suddenly pass as it started and will we go back to the life the way it was before? After a month suspended in history, will we wake up as if from a dream?

My grandmother was born in the 1910s, in a Paris illuminated by street lamps and traveled by carriages; and died in the early 2000s, in a new millennium, a world of wireless telephones, miniskirts, and the internet. Man had been on the moon and a Concorde took three-and-a-half hours to fly from London to New York!

But in reality I, too, born in 1984, saw the world changing in a spiraling way...I was born in a Germany still divided in two, I grew up with telephone booths and appointments to be meticulously met. At school, research was done on encyclopedias, air travel was still a luxury, and video games were not virtual realities but small black and white screens...Now that I am a mother—yours and Leandra's—I live in this new world at high speed, always connected and reachable, with any information available anytime...But I don't really remember how it all happened... maybe it's true that you quickly get used to progress quickly...I went through high school without a smartphone and Wikipedia, I was almost twenty when I got my first digital camera, I wrote my thesis before Facebook...I traveled without Google Maps...My first car didn't even have power steering let alone the GPS! But now all this also seems obvious to me, normal, due. And I really believe that one day you will have technology that seems like science-fiction to me...robots...teleportation, flying machines, space cruises...But how fast can you really go?

Under this moon, always the same, with your breath in my ears, the night is still and motionless...but at this same moment in hospitals all over the world there is noise, there is frenzy, light, speed, noise, tiredness, fear, adrenaline...there is heroism and there is loneliness...there is anger, greed, haste and death.

It is like finding yourself thrown into a novel...life that changes within a few days...In February we celebrated my birthday with an impromptu picnic in the park, remember? Your dad went to get pizza, my parents were there, Leandra playing on the swing, you had just learned to sit on it on your own...and there were people of all kinds around, people chatting, running, taking dogs for a walk...we already knew about China, but just the way we feel about an earthquake, a volcanic eruption, a flood on the other side of the world...we feel it, we're sorry, maybe we make a donation or a charity text message, talk to someone, share a post on social media and then, you forget about it...the information, even if present, slips into the background...the background of your life that continues as before...generally hectic and it doesn't let you pause to reflect, feel empathy...in the newspaper the same news slips from the first page to the internal ones and then generally disappears...and your days continue...

This time, however, after having slipped to the bottom, the news exploded again on the first pages, from China the disease had now arrived here, in Italy, by plane, hidden in the suitcases of tourists and briefcases of businessmen, passed from hand to hand with the money of a tip and the embrace of a child.

The world, as big as it is, now appears smaller and smaller...so, the less political and more natural borders, actually make it as if they were not there...nothing stops the air...nothing stops this subtle disease...perhaps even more sneaky because it doesn't seem so scary... People didn't take it seriously...it seemed like the flu...nobody wanted to have limits imposed, change their habits.

In a moment, however, everything changed...it was like reading something by Orwell...

Different information is given by the minute, scientists attack each other, news is given and then denied. First we all had to stay calm and move on, then suddenly everything had to stop. We must hide from the virus, we must protect those who are less strong, the elderly, the sick, the ones with compromised immune systems...We shut ourselves in our homes because the hospitals are collapsing...

We are sixty-million inhabitants, how can we stop everyone? How can you stop such a fast disease? It seemed impossible, however within a few days schools, cinemas, bookstores, libraries, bars, restaurants, then also shops and part of the factories closed...basically, almost everything...the streets are empty, it is not allowed to go out except to buy groceries or go to work (for those few who still can)...it doesn't seem true...and the strange thing is that we don't know until when? and we don't know what will happen...will our economy survive? Will the concept of united Europe survive? Will we return to free travel as before? Will we be able to hug strangers? How many scars will we carry from these weeks? Even psychologically?

Sometimes people frighten me...public opinion, manipulated, distorted...the anger that arises from this feeling of powerlessness and transforms the minds...the neighbors who report from their windows if they see someone running by themselves through the park or going out more than once with their dog, parents exasperated by their children, social rules, but also personal freedoms dangerously questioned...

We are so lucky...it still seems like a long vacation...dad works from home and suddenly instead of twelve hours a day he works six and has so much more time to be with us...we have a big house and a huge garden, there also is a forest...spring is exploding among the branches and unrolls rugs of daisies...With Leandra we make paper masks, pasta and salt biscuits, jams, drawings...we prepare pizza bread and homemade pasta...

Your sister already misses kindergarten friends, grandparents, dance, lessons, violin...I hope that isolation will end before she really realizes it...I'm afraid to see her face become sad one day, to see her feel in a cage, for us not to be enough for her...

You are still so small, the world to come, whatever it will be, will be "your" world, you will have no memories of the former...yet I cannot imagine what it could be if all this continued and you grew up here, within these walls only with us, without other faces, other stimuli, other children...

I would like to be able to live past the anguish...to be able to see the opportunities of all this...more than to see them, to realize them. Make a contribution to the world that will be. I know, it's easy to have a heart full of hope and gratitude if you have your family next to you, a house with a garden that allows you to breathe the spring, a husband who continues to work for now (even if differently), a garden to grow vegetables, a library full of books, a kitchen full of food...but this is my life, and it's my plate. Whether it is a votive offering or the pot in a poker game, I don't know...I know that I will protect it, but that I will also try to lighten it, to keep its essence, not superficial stuff, I will try to share more...I have traveled and lived in various parts of the world...I have friends and family who have done likewise, loved ones are scattered across the continents, I don't know when I will see them again, if the distances will return to being as big as a century ago, that's okay, even giving up a lot of what I have today and which seems indispensable to me, I know that from the crisis comes the change. Change that is necessary, essential, even positive, but that without crisis we would not have accepted or had time to see.

I look at you in dim light...I smell your scent...I thank heaven that you are no longer in my belly...

I would have been so afraid to give birth now...and instead I have the privilege of being able to be reborn with you, face this new world as you are doing...follow your curious looks, your laughter of enthusiasm, the courage and the wonderful recklessness of going beyond the limits...for you, whose every day is still the first day that brings with it new, brand new perfumes and experiences...learn that you have nothing to lose, but only to explore, to discover, to welcome, and to live! In birth there is the essence of Nature that does not stop...the confidence of life that does not care about the superstructures...The joy that overcomes fear. With each breath you teach me something and it's a joy, after all the noise is gone, to hear you distinctly...a joy to have time. Time to embrace your dad and feel in every fiber of my body that I love him and that together we are like reeds in a pond, that we can bend but we will not break, we can question everything because the essentials are here in our arms and it is you, Orlando and Leandra. Everything will be fine because we are together and in one way or another we will face it...

Riccardo Betti and Johanna Fridrich, married since 2014, are parents of two children, 4½-year-old Leandra and 10-month-old Orlando. Riccardo, a lawyer, is Italian. Johanna, who among many things has been a pastry baker for many years, has a French dad and German mom but has lived in Italy since childhood. Their home is in Umbria, in the midst of greenery, close to their families and Iago, a beautiful black Labrador with a white-faced muzzle.

Sergio Pallottelli is an internationally renowned flutist and teacher based in Houston, an amazing cook, and a dear friend. www.sergiopallottelli.com

Carded at Whole Foods
by Dan Blum

Alright so I'm fifty-eight years old, right? I mean, it's not like I'm forty. So yeah, I tried to get in before eight in the morning with the over-sixty crowd only this supermarket's like soooo unchill!!!! They're all like, "excuse me, you don't look like you're sixty," and I'm like, "I so am sixty, geez, I'm like sixty-one, just ask ANYONE," and they're like, "I'll have to see some ID," and I'm like, "shoot, I left it home. Can I just run inside? My friend's like waiting for me." Because OMFG I'm fifty-eight! I mean close enough, right? And they're like, "No ID, can't let you in," and I'm like, "pretty please? Just this once?" And they're like, "You know the drill. We let you in, we could lose our license." And I'm like, "what*ever*!"

So I call my friend who's this really cool retiree at this totally lit assisted living place in Jersey, and I'm like, "Bro, you won't believe it! I was carded at effing Whole Foods. They say I'm not old enough for the over-sixty hours. I'm fifty-eight! I mean WTF?" And he's like, "I know someone who can fix you an ID no problem," and I'm like, "FR?" and he's like, "yeah," and I'm like, That'd be amazing!"

And so I get this ID and I go back to Whole Foods and guess what? It's the same bouncer at the entrance. This mean-looking guy with these big biceps. So no probs, right? I take out my ID and show it to him. So he studies it and he looks at me and he studies it again and he looks at me again and then he's like, "scuse me" and then he's back with this police officer and I'm like, big yikes, and they're pointing at me and the cop is marching right at me!

Next thing I know I'm in the back of the patrol car and he's lecturing me, like, "You kids think this is just a game?" and I'm like, "No, sir," and he's like, "Sure! I know your kind. You think you can handle it in there, you think you're old enough, you're all grown up?" And I'm like, "No, sir," and he's like, "Well let me tell you something. You're just another punk!" and I'm like "Yes, sir."

Then I'm at the police station calling my son Rob, begging him to come pick me up. I am soooo hosed. I'm like, "Rob? Listen, I got carded at Whole Foods. I'm really, really sorry. Can you come get me? No, I'm not laughing...Yes, I appreciate you...No, I didn't do this to hurt you," and he's like, "That's it. You're grounded," and I'm like, "OhMyGod that's terrible! I'm like crying here. *NOT*. Like dude, it's a pandemic! Everyone's grounded."

Dan Blum is a writer of humor and serious fiction, living in Wellesley, Massachusetts with his family. You can find more of his humor at: www.rottingpost.com

Book Release in a Time of Plague
by Ann Chamberlin

The long-awaited release of my latest book, <u>Clogs and Shawls</u>, a memoir of my English grandmother and her sisters, was scheduled for the end of January 2020. I hired the dance band for the date of my usual launch party and was about to put money down on the venue: the Commander's House in Fort Douglas, Salt Lake, if there's snow on the ground. It's my yard when the weather's good.

Release delayed to the end of February.

I had to postpone the event, since I needed to be in Gold Canyon, Arizona, in February and March for the Arizona Renaissance Festival. In rickety Tudor buildings set amid cactus and dry washes, I own the most wonderful bookstore: everything from how to make your own chain mail to the stitches used in sixteenth-century doublets. And my own titles, too, of course.

It's not hoarding if it's books and if you get to save them from library dumpsters and then share them with fellow readers of eclectic tastes and geeky knowledge. I don't mind seeing them go—to good homes, of course. And I got to own them, even if just for a little.

I get book signers to come to the shop, new faces every weekend, and I put my own new release on the list for mid-March—just to be safe—where I will offer free birthday cake and a look at the title to any of the 17,000 visitors the fair gets on a regular day.

Delay to mid-April.

But if I put a rush order on it, I'm told, I might get a few copies by March 28—my birthday and coincidently the last weekend of the fair.

I place the rush order, ready to pay the extra shipping. The books are printed in China. I move the party date to that last planned weekend of the fair.

Which never actually came.

Up near the festival front gate, where I go to check the mail shed, stands a giant old saguaro cactus that seems to be offering an obscene gesture to the world: one tall, straight branch leaping out of a fist of four tightly clenched other branches. By the sixth weekend of the eight-week run, COVID-19 and general isolation have suddenly become all the news, and the abusive cactus at our gates is no defense, though it stood for live magic tricks against the pixels of blockbuster videos, and for calloused fingers feeling their way through a new tune against a canned drum machine.

"Why are we still open?" asks my friend, the sword-and-whip master, as he stops by the shop on March 15. He is such a popular act. Think Zorro. Many fans want hugs and kisses. They want to rub his hairy chest where it peeks out between shirt laces.

He leaves to isolate in his trailer until his next show time. Okay, if that's the great he-man, touching elbows and pouring over the same books with truly avid patrons is getting a little scary. But how better to enjoy facsimiles of The Book of Kells than side-by-side with a scholar who can describe to you how each curl of illuminating ink was formed?

We're selling a lot of Bocaccio, that collection of ribald Italian tales from the fourteenth-century. Different plague, different isolation. We even have the adults-only Decameron tarot deck, too, which does well. There are a lot of folks in beaked plague-doctor masks; the guy who sells them is making a fortune. People wearing them can't read very well and are not our customers.

We're not making all that much money. The crowd is thin, thinner than the usual Sunday, when people go to church first before hitting the Pirate Pub for their first shot of rum for the day. People are using rum for hand sanitizer no longer on the Walmart shelves.

But still, a book might be just the thing to get you through the next few weeks. I know I'm an anachronism; books, when so few read anything not on their devices.

One of my regular visitors from the cast, in historic character—the fellow who directs readings of my play scripts on a Monday night—likes to pretend he's about to ignite an auto-da-fé with my stock. "Readers!" he always exclaims with disgust, although in truth a great reader himself. "You'll be the death of monarchy."

I watch a little tyke in a pink taffeta princess dress and plastic tiara on askew wag her finger at him. She clings to the picture book about dragons soon to become hers, and tells him it's still okay—no, vitally important, in fact--to read. It's her right, and she will.

My inquisitor is disarmed and laughs out loud with the youngster. "You go for it, girl."

To read books, not to press the Down arrow through throw-away content. Cover to cover. To follow a book-length argument or intricate plot. To hold your finger on page 10 and compare it to 245 when scrolling on a screen you'd get lost, and then you'd decide it wasn't as important as the next screen you can click on, and all continuity is lost.

Vitally important. For one more generation. Perhaps.

Or is it?

Near the end of that Sunday afternoon, a collector comes and wants the hundred-year-old Plutarch set, but I'm too frazzled to find all the volumes. He says he can't come back another weekend; he's worried about his elderly mother. I promise to mail it to him when I find the strays. He insists he will read all nine volumes cover to cover. He just may do that. A builder of movie sets, he now has the time.

My shop assistant finishes helping yet another patron straggling in denial on this last outing in a stolen day of sunshine. They were pouring over a copy of Heston Blumenthal's history of the feasting of the English upper class, complete with intricate recipes and fantastic pictures. It's too expensive for either of them, food and book. And sharing food with strangers, even friends, has become deadly. But together they could dream.

My assistant returns behind the counter. He knows he stood closer than he should have. He works security when he's not a book seller and gets a lot of books read in his little shack.

"Why don't they close down, already?" he asks when the front of the shop is briefly empty. Another he-man, looking pale.

At five p.m., two strangers march in to claim the red-and-white Lego queen in our leaded-glass window. She's part of a treasure hunt kids can play, with all thirty-one acres of the fair as their playground. You find all four figures, you get a prize at the end of the day.

Actually, the strangers scurry through the bodies in the shop. The strangers have jobs that usually keep them at a distance from patrons. To

30

retrieve the figures, they have to plunge into the toxic stream where we've been bathing with happy, welcoming faces all day. The Lego queen vanishes before I've quite figured out what's happening.

"That's it," my assistant says, slapping his large, scarred, knife-throwing hands (yes, he also does that for a living) on the counter. "The first sure sign that we're closing."

I don't get another sign. Management doesn't want to admit they stayed open too long, and they would have to if they actually sent us a letter or an email.

I learn what I can around the whip master's fire that night as—out of our skirts and tight bodices, doublets and hose, and back in jeans and t-shirts—we roast the last of the marshmallows and squish them with chocolate between graham crackers. Is the preferred method to burn the marshmallows to a crisp, or carefully watch them until they're just brown? The old argument rages between more somber discussion.

Those who usually limit themselves to one s'more a night don't stop until all the makings are gone. Comfort food. Then we eat the remaining stale crackers, dry, chased by the whip master's signature tequila, until they're all gone, both the cracker box and the bottle, empty.

The fire dies. (It runs on propane; the whip master just turns a knob. Real fires would be too dangerous.)

It's no use quarantining against these people, my family two months out of the year. We all shower in the same grubby bath house. We've been hugging for weeks. We all went out and put on a show for people in plague-doctor masks. If one of us has it, we all have it now. There are at least a thousand of us.

We've closed two weeks early. What will the rennies do? (Rennies, the jargon term for those who move across the country, renfaire to renfaire. Ren for renaissance, if you still don't get it. Kind of like carnies.) The campground, where some live in tents prone to blowing away when wind comes off the saguaro, is closing with less than a week to pack up and make other arrangements. That's two weeks without pay, pay that is never enough to set anything by. The festivals they were going to, to pitch tents again, have already said they will not open. My roommate will park her leaky camper in her mother's driveway in Texas until... Until whatever happens.

Everyone is frantic on their phones. Until their plans run out.

Monday morning, I cancel the express order for <u>Clogs and Shawls</u>. There will be no cake, no festive signing. There'll be nobody here in the desert to receive the shipment. I won't get to see my books until I'm home, if I make it home. I am in the at-risk category. Launch will come online and by mail only.

"Come stay a week or so in my little house up in Chloride, Arizona," invites the whip master's partner. "We'll play Scrabble and backgammon. We'll tell stories. It'll be just like the Decameron."

I would love to. "Just let me pack the shop up." But at 6:15 a.m. on Wednesday, my phone, which thinks I'm still in Utah, tells me to duck and cover because there's been an earthquake. My son, who's been laid off, and my husband, whose care center has wisely not allowed visitors for two weeks, need me. Chloride will have to wait.

I just hugged my roommates good-bye. The silence of the desert is all around me, mourning doves coo and, at night, coyotes howl and owls hoot at each other on the roof over my head. I have forty-eight more hours before my ride comes, bringing the truck we must pack up before the treacherous two-day drive of motels and drive-up restaurants. Of coughing old men and their walkers bumping me as they cross the six-foot separation lines they can't see as they desperately grab for the last soda can in the cooler at the drug store.

It is a long, long, empty drive, part of it across the Navajo Nation. But my friend who works in the Navajo Nation Department of Justice and who had to cancel lunch as she scrambled to keep her people safe, tells me they already have twenty-three cases on the reservation. And they haven't been in denial as long as we have been amid jousts and turkey legs.

At least I have a home to go to. A garden where the plum trees will be blooming, encircling the isolation lot with white fairy breath.

But now, it's just me in the apartment over my quiet, locked-up bookshop that will have to wait until next year—or ever?—to have <u>Clogs and Shawls</u> on its shelves.

At least it is a bookstore. Downstairs... Well, the Plutarch is gone. Who'd have thought I'd miss the Plutarch? We sold out of the Bocaccios. But in this silence, silence I always long for in my usually busy days, I do have enough literature to fill the rest of my life, even if the truck never comes.

The Moriscos of Spain? Or shall I tackle Kabbalah?

Water's running low, and I know there's no more in the store. My eyes are puffy when I wake in the morning. The internet tells me puffy eyes are just allergies. All the dust, swirling in the empty campground around me.

The computer always beats me at Scrabble. It doesn't know what any of these words mean.

Then the internet shuts down. The power is iffy. The privies are foul.

I try to plan my book release strategy with all these new constraints but have lost the heart to do so.

Do you remember the Twilight Zone episode where the world ends, and the librarian who somehow survives rejoices? No pesky patrons will come to interrupt his reading pleasure now.

And then his glasses break, and there's no one to fix them.

Ann Chamberlin is author of nineteen books, including The Book of Wizzy *and, just released,* Clogs and Shawls. *annchamberlin.com*

2021
by David Cowley (United Kingdom)

As I drew back the curtains the bright morning sun flooded the room with light. The sky was cloudless and deep blue, the kind of sky you see in the mountains, high above the treeline. Judging by the silver dusting of frost on the car roofs, the night had been clear too, the temperature below freezing.

A year ago most of those cars would have been gone by now, people driving children to school or setting out on the daily commute, going about their business. Nowadays though, everything was at a standstill.

A lone airplane crossed the sky, its vapour trail a blasphemous gash across the pure blue. It would be a government flight – food, medical supplies or, perhaps, military personnel. No one else was flying these days.

It was exactly a year since the Prime Minister, studiously avoiding the use of the word "lockdown" on the advice of behavioural psychologists, had announced that he was locking down the whole country. Mostly this was met with resignation rather than shock, acceptance rather than outrage. A few lone voices in politics and big business had sputtered indignantly about individual freedom and damage to the economy but they were swiftly silenced. Social pressure and, in some cases, newly passed legislation saw to that.

The initial three week order was extended and extended again, until it became indefinite. What had begun as a temporary measure became a way of life.

The food riots in London, in the summer of 2020, and reports of organised crime moving in on the food supply, led to the imposition of martial law. A newly established government of national unity introduced rationing of food and other essentials. Supermarkets and warehouses were converted into food distribution centres, guarded by soldiers. Cities were divided into zones and a strict curfew imposed. Anyone caught in breach of the rules risked internment without trial and looters could be shot on sight.

By late November, the spread of the disease had begun to slow. Hopes rose that the virus was on the wane. In a new climate of optimism, government cautiously eased restrictions in the run up to Christmas. Within a fortnight the number of cases had started to rise again. Controls were swiftly re-imposed and, by the end of January, daily life was more constrained than ever.

With weapons to fight it already proving elusive, the virus had started to mutate rapidly, becoming more virulent. Acquired immunity provided uncertain levels of protection.

The health system was overwhelmed. My son was a doctor in a large, London hospital. Although we lived less than 20 miles apart, I hadn't seen him in over a year. Working impossibly long shifts, often without adequate protective gear, he was soon stricken with the virus. He was one of the lucky ones. His survival had seemed almost miraculous but he had insisted on returning to work as soon as he was able. I admired his courage more than I could say, but feared for him constantly.

The hunt for a vaccine, or even effective treatments, always seemed to be two steps behind. Only stringent social isolation was limiting the spread of disease.

Real life slowed to a crawl. Governments the world over abandoned economic orthodoxy, emptying their coffers to fight the disease, prop up economies and maintain social order. The work force was cut back to essential services. Things that could went online; everything else just stopped.

It was boom-time for the technology companies. Their tendrils reached ever more deeply into every corner of our lives. There were even rumours on social media about a top secret artificial intelligence project which would oversee global social and economic policy, the prospect of a new high-tech utopia rising from the ashes of a ravaged world.

As I looked out of the window, my musings were brusquely interrupted by a text notification. It was the government sending me my weekly outdoor authorisation and food collection code.

An hour later, an empty rucksack on my back, I stepped out of my apartment into the chilly, spring day. I walked slowly down the street, savouring the fresh air and the tepid warmth of the sun on my face. Ahead of me was a checkpoint. Two heavily armed policemen in navy blue hazmat suits watched me approach.

"Good morning, sir. Can I see your authorisation, please," said the taller of the two men, his voice muffled by his face mask.

I presented my phone and he scanned the code. There was a short pause then a beep.

"I'm sorry, but this hasn't gone through," he said.

I felt a stab of fear. I was in no doubt that, behind the policeman's courtesy, stood the unforgiving might of the state. To be caught outside without authorisation was a serious offence. Things went wrong sometimes and I had heard of innocent people being interned.

He re-scanned the code and this time it registered.

"Sorry about that, sir. System's been playing up a bit this morning. You're good to go. Just make sure you come back through this checkpoint on your way home."

As I reached the food collection centre, I joined the long, widely spaced queue. Two soldiers, in biological warfare suits, looked idly on. Some people were engrossed in their phones, a few engaged in subdued conversation. Most were silent, anxious to be back in the safety of their homes.

When my turn came, I placed my phone under the scanner and, after a short pause, the hatch opened to reveal a plastic crate full of government defined essentials – my weekly allowance of food and household goods. Transferring them quickly to the rucksack, I placed the crate in the sterilisation bay and headed back to the check point.

Once through, I glanced at my watch. I had forty-five minutes left before I was obliged by law to be back home. I turned onto the tree-lined footpath leading uphill into a small wood.

At one time the roar of traffic from the nearby motorway would have intruded on this haven of natural beauty but today the copse was alive with birdsong. Hidden somewhere in the trees, a woodpecker hammered industriously.

I loved this corner of the zone. It was good to feel unpaved earth beneath my feet, smell the damp fragrance of woodland and hear the gentle susurration of the breeze in the trees. We were almost into April and the first soft green leaves were smudging the stark outline of the bare branches, a reminder that life would go on regardless of the fate of humanity.

As I emerged from the wood, a small police drone swooped down and hovered a few feet in front of me. I stood still to let its face recognition software cross-check my identity with my outdoor authorisation. Overstaying the permitted two hours by a few minutes meant a fine, longer and you faced arrest.

As the drone flew away, I checked my watch again. I still had ten minutes. Walking down the hill towards my apartment, I could see the coils of barbed wire marking the southern perimeter of the zone. Beyond that was a no man's land of empty pasture with a small stream running through it. In one corner of the field a tractor was beginning to plough the land, which had recently been requisitioned in time for spring planting.

Reluctantly I climbed the stairs to my apartment, daunted by the prospect of another week alone, only my phone and laptop linking me to friends and family.

After unpacking my rucksack I made coffee and, settling on the settee, switched on the television to catch up on the news. I was surprised to see the Prime Minister, solemn and sober-suited, speaking from behind a lectern.

"And so I can, today, announce that a programme of vaccination will be rolled out with immediate effect, starting with health and other essential workers but extending to every man, woman and child in the United Kingdom. The same will be happening in the next few days across the entire world."

I could hardly believe what I was hearing. Did this really mean the tables were turning in this strange war against an invisible enemy?

"Needless to say, the global production, distribution and administration of this vaccine represents the biggest logistical exercise ever undertaken in the history of mankind, so I must ask you, please, to be patient. Each and every one of you will receive, in due course, notification of the place and time of your vaccination, but I must warn you that any person attempting to jump the queue will face the full force of the law.

"As soon as possible, we will lift restrictions on social contact and travel within the United Kingdom. We will work with other countries to ensure that, in the long term, we will, once again, be free to travel overseas and resume full economic activity. However, we must also take this opportunity to look long and hard at the way we go about our daily lives. In this, our moment of hope, let us remember that a crisis of this magnitude brings not only danger but also opportunity. Let us not forget, before this emergency, we were already facing the dual challenge of climate change and the pollution of our land, sea and air. We must seize this opportunity to forge a better..."

My phone rang. It was my son.

"Dad, did you hear the news? We've done it. The vaccine works. We're going to beat the virus."

He was exultant. At the sound of his voice something inside of me released and tears ran, unbidden, down my face. I wept for the months of gnawing anxiety and for the way of life we had once taken for granted. I wept for the millions lost along the way and for the pain their loss had brought to countless others. Above all, though, I wept for our salvation and with hope for the future.

After retiring from a distinguished career as principal oboist with the BBC National Orchestra of Wales, David is now fulfilling a long held ambition to study creative writing.

The Pandemic Cleanse: 5 Steps to a Happier Future
by Mia Bella D'Augelli

The 2020 *Out-of-Work Musician's* * *Dictionary* definition of pandemic: "a cleanse for the spirit." *(*Note: if you are not a musician, replace any musical reference that follows to match your career.)*

To get ready for the pandemic cleanse, lie on your couch. Pillows, blankets, the whole comfy cocoon. Have something waiting for you; warm milk, a beer, a pint of ice cream, whatever you had on the five days out of the past year that you took the time to relax.

You're not physically sick, but your mind has been spasming for years. Sometimes you think you're crazy, sometimes you can't believe how lucky you are, sometimes you have no idea what you want in life. It's time to treat yourself.

If you can't afford to take this break, go get a job.

Oh wait, you aren't qualified for anything else, so you should try this five-step self-personalized program. A happier future awaits.

You will be your own all-in-one wellness guru, performance coach, doctor, and psychologist. From the comfort of your own couch, you will turn your life around today with the pandemic cleanse. And best of all, it's free.

--

Step One: Fall Apart.

You don't know what is going on or what to do with yourself. Your career is over for the foreseeable future, so stop striving. Everything you've aimed toward your whole life is on hiatus, and you are too. This cleanse is a public performance purge.

Don't worry about being productive. Let yourself fall apart and take this initial break for a few days, a week, or even longer. No answering emails, touching your instrument, booking concerts, promoting concerts, studying scores. Instead, find things to replace your career. Options include TV, video games, books, exercise, food, chasing a squirrel up a tree, that art project you meant to start ten years ago. Things you can obsess about. Or, simply watch three movies in a row because they're right in front of you on Netflix.

You might start to feel guilty. This is normal. You are used to knowing your schedule and exactly what you need to focus on to succeed with your commitments.

For now, you're in charge of the only thing that matters: your mind. So, numb yourself for a bit while you deal internally with this devastating temporary loss of your livelihood.

The pandemic cleanse is a replacement for those vacations you always said you'd take at home, when instead you agreed to play gigs because saying no is hard and someone offered you money.

If you decide it's time to move on to some soul-searching, now is the time for Step Two. If you're enjoying your time immensely, though, just skip ahead to Step Five.

Step Two: Ask Yourself Lots of Questions.

What are you afraid of? What is your relationship with each fear? Does it deserve your deep care and future energy?

Leave the questioning of your place in the universe for later. If you want to attack it now, prepare to hunker down and think for a while between unpredictable bouts of doubt and tears.

Check on your fear every morning if you are if you are waking up anxious. In fact, do this anytime uncomfortable emotions rise up. Since you have time on your hands, you might as well deal with your problems. Perhaps the exploration is not enjoyable, but it's for the good of your spirit.

You might consider starting a meditation habit, reading one of the self-help books on your shelf, or getting really inebriated and talking with a friend about your woes. If your friend has work in the morning, keep it short and spread out your complaints over several conversations.

Once you've internally asked all the questions you can think of and processed the emotions that welled up, it's time to move on.

Step Three: Make a List of What You Care About.

Unfurl it over a few days, between binging seasons of your new favorite show or after afternoon naps.

Remember, this is what you used to only dream of, a break. Forced rest might not be what you imagined a break to be, but here it is. This pandemic cleanse fell in your lap. Finish it.

So, what do you need in this life? What entrances you? Year after year, what do you want to dive into?

It's okay if music isn't at the top of the list. Other aspects of life are important, too. More important, even. Maybe you're burnt out. But if there's a piece of music that makes your mind feel like it's on fire, listen to it on repeat. (For me, ten days into the cleanse, it was Alfred Shnittke's Trio-Sonata, an arrangement by Yuri Bashmet of Schnittke's 1985 String Trio.)

If money comes to mind, ignore it. You'll never be rich, probably never even comfortably well-off enough that being sick isn't a burden, so remember, there is more to life than retirement. If you have student loans or medical debt, keep on hoping it'll disappear at some point. It's fake money, anyway.

Alternately, you could decide that making money is the most important thing and establish online content as the new be-all and end-all of your productivity. You might become the newest online celebrity and go viral after learning how to use TikTok. You might do nightly livestreamed performances. You might get in touch with every single Facebook friend you have, tell them the horror that your life has become, and get them to support you online. Or maybe you've gotten tired of talking to people digitally already and need a break from screens.

Whenever your cares are narrowed down to the elements that make your heart soar, it's time for Step Four.

Step Four: Migrate Toward Your Cares.

Each day, take something on your list of cares and sink into it. Follow all the paths you can, at least those that don't involve physical contact with other people.

Did you decide you cared about your family? Call them and keep them company while they deal with the same questions you are. This also applies to your close friends. Not everyone is a hermit who wants nothing more than to be left alone for months while the world takes a deep breath. They're freaked out, too.

Have you always wanted to compose a symphony or write a novel or paint a masterpiece? Yes? Start small and make things that suck first. You'll get there soon.

Did you figure out that relaxing is everything you need? Sleep until noon every day, then. Watch all the movie marathons you want, read all the page-turners, just take it easy. Jeez!

Now it's time for the last bit of your journey inward.

Step five: Continue on Your New Path.

You're alive? Well then, your pandemic cleanse was a success. Bravo!

Mia Bella D'Augelli is a violinist and composer who writes to explore the intersection of nature, technology, music, and the mind. www.musicmiabella.com

Some Late-Night Thoughts
(slightly saturated with music, politics, and gin)
by Robert Debbaut

The cacophony of emotional human voices rose from the television[1] and its polyphony was glorious. Not necessarily glorious in the partisan expression that was uttered, but rather in the joy and ecstasy present in that utterance. By contrast, when simultaneously considering the thoughts of the late Lewis Thomas[2], whose mind was clouded with death—his own impending death and the symbolic death he finds within Mahler's Ninth Symphony—one finds him looking into and shuddering away from his perception of the cacophonous and chaotic abyss before which mankind stands. These very real fears were present in Thomas' yesterday as well as our today. Distanced from those days of reading and writing about his reflective essay by some thirty-six years has given me pause to connect Thomas' thesis--one of our shared and absolute horror at the prospective nuclear annihilation of mankind--to the contemporary rampant onslaught of the deadly COVID-19 virus.

Dr. Thomas associates mankind's fears of the Cold War's potential horrors with features of Mahler's epic final symphony and its deeply emotional, even funereal tones. I understand Thomas' fearful pessimism, for at his age, he had lived through the Second World War, the Korean War, the Vietnam War, and the contemporary horrors of both Lebanon,[3] and El Salvador. [4] During his lifetime Thomas had

---

1   The 1984 Democratic National Convention was on the television as I was writing this assignment for a summer seminar on Mahler's symphonies.

2   Lewis Thomas. Late Night Thoughts on Listening to Mahler's Ninth Symphony. Penguin Books. New York, 1995. Lewis Thomas (1913-1993) was an American author, educator, and physician. He was Dean of both the Yale Medical School and the New York University School of Medicine. He is the author of six books on subjects mainly biological, ecological, and medical. Rockefeller University awards the Lewis Thomas Prize to a scientist for artistic achievement.

3   The Lebanese Civil War began in February 1984; our embassy in Beirut was attacked by a suicide bomber that September.

4   A civil war also began in El Salvador in 1984, with the United States spending more than one billion dollars to prop up a brutal military dictatorship there

witnessed the shift of our own government's position on war and militarism go from our shared endeavor to save the world for democracy (idealism) to attempts to sway the public through blatant falsehoods to join a crusade to control the world and to shape it as their own (selfism). Perhaps he believed that the picture we once painted of the Soviets was akin to psychological projection, that being a reflection of our own selfish desires for a "Novus Ordo Seclorum."[5] In seeking an escape from life's inevitable demise Thomas yearned for the opportunity of an escape into music as a refuge from the prospect of nuclear holocaust.

This COVID-19 virus, however, seems to be more analogous to a set of variations than to Mahler's epic and, as Thomas suggests, pessimistic picture of our impending apocalypse. More like Beethoven's compositions than Mahler's, COVID-19 started with a germ motive, one might suggest as virally analogous to the common cold. As with many first variations a solid impression of the theme remains, though just a bit more ornate. Like many such compositions, variation one follows the course of many a common upper respiratory virus. The second variation becomes more ornate, decorating the "theme" (symptoms) with new color. We could follow this strain on and on, but anyone familiar with musical variations certainly gets the point. The problem with COVID-19 is that it has three possible alternative endings: recovery, lasting impairment of the lungs, or death. Thus, unlike the certainty of the end of Mahler 9, COVID-19's last variant will be either happy, sad, or uncertain. It is noteworthy to mention, however, that with the exception of his *Coriolanus* Overture, all of Beethoven's symphonies, concertos, overtures, and his only opera, *Fidelio*, end both positive and triumphant!

While I can see a link between Lewis Thomas' pessimism in the face of such immense, uncontrollable global forces seemingly hell-bent on mutually assured destruction and my own uncertainty of which ultimate variant of COVID-19 may infect me and my fellow human

---

5   "New World Order," or "New Order of the Ages." Did you know it's on our money?

beings, I cannot agree with his premise that music should merely be the escape route of the young (or old, for that matter). Music should be the method by which we enhance communication between our diverse societies and to embrace truth. The exchange of ambassadors with the former Soviet Union, when those ambassadors only managed to heighten the tensions already present between two governments and cultures, ultimately served no common good. On the other hand, an exchange of cultural groups, such as Native American and Russian folk groups, American and Russian artistic organizations, and groups of biological scientists provided the prospect of gaining mutual respect and understanding. Only by the peoples of each society endeavoring to understand one another can we hope to step back from the precipice. The analogy with COVID-19 is that rather than place blind faith in any politician's self-serving proclamation of a divinely-given scientific prowess, it is scientists who should be given full charge over saving the human race from this disease. Effectively fighting this virus is about surviving a pandemic with biological origins and potential scientific and medical solutions, not about winning elections.

Likewise, in these days of "social distancing," music should enhance our daily lives, should be shared with one's fellow "quarantinis" to preserve our sense of connectedness, our very human sameness, our deepest feelings of empathy for our human collective, and to offer others reassurance in the face of such dire consequences. We know not what ultimate variation shall befall any of us, but we can help to make the journey less arduous and stressful for our families and neighbors.

Music, as an act of communication, not as an act of escape, should be both goal and method of the young, and of us all. Denying the attempt of government to usurp the will to live and the urge to create is to deny them the opportunity to inflict a modern feudalism on their people, to invoke a new "Dark Ages," and to break the human spirit. Music of hope and vision, not music of desperation and dissolution, should be both our method of communication and our communion. We must look to the future realistically, yet optimistically if we are, indeed, to have a future. As Mahler did, our composers should seek to regenerate the human spirit through music and to raise our levels of consciousness, both individual and collective. We should reject both the banal music of militarism and nihilism, and embrace a new vision for our society, not through escape into our subconscious, but by its liberation.

The many Lewis Thomases of the world, both historical and contemporary, who see our world clouded by either their own proximity to death or fear of their own uncertain futures, should be comforted by the young. While we experience this time of collective anxieties, one hopes--and even needs--to feel that the young still possess a vision of the future that does not include an escape into regression, into depression, nor into a paralyzing fear of self-annihilation. This was true during the Cold War, and should be now as we wait in the shadow of this virus. An escape into ourselves would only further serve to fragment an already splintered collective consciousness and to cast doubt on our shared existence and survival. It is our collective responsibility to unite mankind and to follow the pathway carved by the young. It is their vision of our future that provides comfort and solace to the aged.

The thesis of Jonathan Schell's "The Unconquerable World"[6] concerns the inability of imperialists, tyrants and despots throughout history to overcome the innate and irrepressible desire of all men for freedom. The lies we have been told, even taught, throughout our lives have been articulated to control us for the purpose of fulfilling the selfish interests of those in power. We have been told that we must defend our "freedom" by compromising and usurping the freedom of some falsely identified "enemy." Be it for fear of nuclear annihilation or of an infectious pandemic we must not allow this to happen. To concede this defeat by actual or would-be authoritarians is to allow either a symbolic or an actual viral and nuclear winter to cloud the sunshine of

---

6   Jonathan Schell. The Unconquerable World: Power, Nonviolence, and the Will of the People. Metropolitan Books. Henry Holt and Company. New York, 2003.

enlightenment, and ultimately result in mankind's creative and psychological regression. Remember this, my friends: Music and Art are about truth.

Robert Debbaut is an American conductor who has led orchestras in Asia, Europe, and North America. (This essay, is an adaptation of one written in 1984.) robertdebbaut.wordpress.com

What Goes on at Whitney Mountain
by Victoria Dougherty

Hopely, Virginia

The drive to the Habersham's seems like forever, and now I'm sure that it really does take Easter every bit of an hour to get to school, like I heard. It's above freezing again, and while the pavement is wet and there's still plenty of snow on the ground, the streets are okay, and even the dirt road we have to turn down in order to get to Easter's isn't so bad. There's just a lot of mud and puddles trimmed with a thin lacing of ice.

"Pretty out here," I say to Easter, and she sort of purses her lips and smiles as best she can. Tapping the toe of her cowboy boot, she sits on her hands and looks out the window.

Easter lives at the foot of Whitney Mountain, which is one of the smaller mountains in the range – one my dad says is hardly a mountain at all. There's no mailbox at the base of Easter's driveway, just a big, white wooden cross with "Jesus Saves" printed on it in bold, black paint. There's a wreath of plastic, crimson flowers hung where the two slats of wood intersect. Dad pulls up in front of the house and jerks his parking brake into place.

Easter's house is old. Probably more than a hundred years, which isn't uncommon in these parts. But it's not old in a charming, historic home sort of way, like on my mom's street in town. Easter's house is barely-standing old. But it does have dignity. There aren't dogs under the porch and the lawn isn't littered with the carcasses of rusted Chevys, like some of the homes we passed to get here. Those embodied every cliché of the mountain poor, from the flowered sheets serving as curtains, to the duct tape that holds together cracked windows, and the saddest, most crooked swing sets you'll ever lay eyes on. A few of those homes were trailers and they were actually the nice ones, despite what some people like to say about trailers and those who inhabit them.

Comparatively, Easter's home is nice, too. It doesn't look good, but it does look neat and cared for. The roof is patched with mismatched tiles, but the holes are fixed and smoke puffs out of her chimney, so at least I know she'll be warm. There's a structure a few yards from the back door that could be a shed or an outhouse. I rather think it's the latter.

"Do you want Twila to walk you up to the door, honey?" Dad asks her. And I'm so glad he did, because I didn't have the nerve.

"No," Easter says. "I mean, no thank you."

I smile at her and she smiles back. Not quite so uncomfortable this time.

"I'm really glad you spent the night," I tell her and I mean it and want her to know that, even if neither of us really had a choice about it.

"Me, too," she says and I like that she appears to mean it as well.

"Oh, and don't forget this." I pass Easter my old laptop, which still works just fine. "Use it as long as you like. I don't need it or anything."

"Thanks," she says.

If she's embarrassed, she doesn't show it, and that's a relief. It's probably more embarrassing for her to have to sign out a laptop at school every day and in front of everyone. It's not like kids are mean about it, it's just that at a school like Putnam, which is pretty much *the* school for gifted kids, the student body tends to be financially secure. Okay, let's just say it – rich.

Easter was plucked out of her crap public county school when her test scores made it clear she didn't belong there. But she doesn't really belong at Putnam either. Socially, I mean. I know that sounds awful, but it doesn't mean people don't like her. They do! I do! It's just, well, like my dad says, "Easter has grown up on a different planet than you, and it can't be easy for her."

That became abundantly clear when the county bus crashed in the sleet storm yesterday, and Easter's mom told her that she was just going to have to figure out how she was going to get home for herself. It's only on account of Dad and me stopping to pick up takeout at Dim Sum Yu Lose Sum, where Easter works, that we found out about her predicament. She was actually going to hitchhike back to Hopely, but Dad said, "No way! You're coming with us, quarantine or not."

Of course, none of this really matters now. I mean, with the boomer remover going around, school will probably be cancelled for the remainder of the year.

"Hey, don't forget your lunch," I say.

Easter climbs out of Dad's Prius, arms balancing a Jenga tower of school books, plus my old laptop and the turkey and avocado sandwich my dad's girlfriend made for her. A big-sounding dog starts to bark just as she turns to face her house, and some guy flies out the front door, slamming it hard with his boot. He's holding a little baby close, and that's the only gentle thing about him. Otherwise, he radiates the kind of rage you only see in a comic book villain. Like Clive Tuggle in *Zombie Apocalypse*, who's calm on the outside, but on the inside it's like he just swallowed a nuclear missile, and at some point, sometime, it's going to blow.

"Hunter," Easter says under her breath.

So, that must be Hunter Caine, her sister's boyfriend. He's not what I expected, I have to say. Not at all how Easter described him, although admittedly Easter didn't say all that much except that she hates him. Hunter Caine is tall and thin, with one of those half grown-in mustaches, and he's got just about the brightest eyes I've ever seen. They burn orange like a Hawaiian sunset and would make him beautiful if it wasn't for the look on his face. That alone makes me understand why Easter thinks he's such an asshole.

Bonnie, Easter's sister, runs out of the house next, and her whole face is red and wet.

"Get back here!" She screams, and it's like a horror movie scream. "Or I swear to God I'm gonna call the police this time!"

Hunter Caine pivots and freezes—so do the rest of us, if I'm going to tell the truth. Because when he turns, we see he's got this big, serrated knife tucked into his belt! Only Dad has the nerve to move, and opens the door to his car, getting out leg by leg and standing up carefully.

"Hey, kids," he says. "Is there anything I can do to help here?"

"You can stay out of our business," Hunter says.

"I'm not trying to interfere," Dad explains. "I just want to know if there's anything I can do? Is Dora home?"

And that's kind of a shocker, because I didn't know that Dad was on a first-name basis with Easter's mother.

As if on cue, Dora, Bonnie and Easter's mom, opens the screen door and steps out of the house. Her blonde hair is down and frayed at the ends, like she hasn't had a chance to brush it yet. She's got a cigarette in hand. "You might as well just turn the fuck around, Hunter, because you're not goin' anywhere with that little baby girl," she says.

That little baby girl is awfully quiet and that in and of itself adds a whole other creep-factor to this scenario. Seems to me a baby should be crying when her parents are at each other's throats. With this one, it's as if she's waiting things out, seeing what's going to happen. Or maybe she's just scared to death.

I look over at Easter, and she's holding her books and things so tightly that her knuckles have gone white. It looks like she's going to cry and I feel terribly for her. We're all just waiting for Hunter Caine to do something and none of us has any clue as to what that something is going to be. He seems the type who's capable of just about anything.

But Hunter takes a deep breath and bites down on his bottom lip. He looks down at his baby and it's impossible to say what he might be thinking. Then, without a word, he turns around and walks past Bonnie and Dora, marching right back into the house. Bonnie runs after him, calling, "Hun! Hun!" Dora takes a very deep drag off of her cigarette and nods to my dad.

"Everything okay?" he asks Easter's mom.

"No," she says.

Dora walks over to Easter and takes the sandwich and laptop off her hands.

"You thank Mr. Black?"

"She sure did," Dad says. "It was a pleasure to have her. We hope she'll come again soon. Maybe after all this craziness is over."

Dora drops her cigarette in a paw-print shaped mini-puddle and smacks her lips. They're stained a bright coral, as if she just tried on some lipstick that didn't suit her and wiped it off with a tissue. She leans over and kisses Easter on the forehead like she's the only good thing in her life, then puts her arm around her. They start heading back into the house, too.

In the window, I can see Bonnie's hands flailing as she talks to that boyfriend of hers. "Talks" is the polite way of putting it. She looks like she's begging and pleading and it's awful to watch. Especially since he's just standing there stiff, letting her tire herself out. All the time, he's clutching their baby to his chest, like she's his possession and his alone. Finally, Bonnie collapses into a chair, and that's when Hunter Caine very tentatively gives her their baby to hold. At least he's trying, I guess.

I am not going to lie. It's really strange to see a boy and girl who are only a year older than me taking care of a baby. A baby that's their own! The kids in their year at Putnam are getting ready to take SATs, planning trips to visit colleges, and plotting their futures. Bonnie Habersham and Hunter Caine seem to have a hard enough time just getting through the day, let alone thinking about what might be tomorrow or next year.

We start home and Dad and I don't say much for some time. Just a comment here and there about the way the clouds are curling around the mountains and how deep some of the potholes are out here. When we turn onto a street with a real name and not just a route number, Dad breaks our silence.

"You know, girls like Easter," he says. "Her family doesn't get meat from the grocery store. They can't afford that with a new baby in the house. Not to mention the costs of having Easter in a school like Putnam. They get their meat on the mountain, in their backyard – squirrels, possums, rabbits. Did you see the knife that young man was carrying?"

It's good to learn Hunter Caine was carrying that knife for food procurement and not something more sinister, but it doesn't feel all that great to learn they can't afford to go to the butcher.

"I thought Easter was on a scholarship."

"I don't mean the tuition, but all the extras. The school supplies, the field trips. Better clothes, so that Easter doesn't stick out like a sore thumb."

"Aren't there charities that could help them out?" I ask.

Dad nods. "Dora's too proud to go to the food bank. She works two jobs, you know. Or at least she did before all of this started."

I think about how many times I've seen Billie, our cafeteria lady, and Easter finishing up breakfast together in commons, just as I arrive at school. I figured Easter had breakfast with Billie because she got to school so much earlier than most of us due to taking the county bus. Now I feel like a complete idiot for not realizing that Easter doesn't have breakfast at home because she doesn't *have* breakfast at home. The homemade pancakes at our house must have seemed pretty extravagant to her.

"You okay?" my dad asks.

I shake my head. "Not really."

Once I say that, I start to cry. I can't stop, so my dad just pulls over and holds me. He's so good at that and I find myself hoping that Easter has someone to hold her right now. Dora's got her hands full with Bonnie and that baby, and can't have much left over for her youngest. And Hunter Caine. He seems to need someone to hold him most of all. Because maybe if he had that, he'd stop holding that little girl of his in the way he does.

Victoria Dougherty is the author of Cold War thrillers The Bone Church, Welcome to the Hotel Yalta, *and* The Hungarian. *Her epic fantasy romance series, including* Savage Island *and the forthcoming* Breath, *are her newest works of fiction.*
www.victoriadoughertybooks.com

Last Night
by Gerald Elias

At this point, it's too late for false modesty. You know who I am. The big name draw in Vegas, in Paris, London, New York. The biggest. Platinum all the way, baby. I play the piano. I sing. You name it. If it's been written, I play it in my own inimitable style. I've got a better voice than Tom Jones ever had and I play piano better than Hamlisch ever could. I don't dance. Dancing's for wannabes. I banter with the crowd. The fancy outfits, the techno fireworks, the bevy of scantily clad beauties. It makes for one splashy show.

I've also gained notoriety for leading what's called an "extravagant" lifestyle by polite society. Impolite society might call it "wanton" or "dissolute," which it has on more than one occasion. Mere value judgements, I say. Mostly envy, I suspect. Free from the encumbrances of a wife and kids, it has been reported—with revealing full color photographs in the choicest gossip magazines--that I live life to the fullest. Publicity like that only helps. All in all, no one can beat my marketability on the entertainment circuit. No one. I get about a hundred requests a day to play at fund-raising events for humanitarian causes, because when Mr. and Mrs. Bigpockets see my name on an invitation, Mrs. Bigpockets sends the RSVP pronto and Mr. Bigpockets opens his checkbook. I'm as household a name as Kleenex. I turn down almost every request, not because I don't appreciate the value of the causes or the sincerity of the people behind them but, frankly, because there are only twenty-four hours in a day, and life is just too damn short. You will soon see how ironic a statement that is, because of an offer I did accept. Like they said in the Godfather, it was an offer I couldn't refuse. An offer from the Lysen's Disease Foundation. If only.

A young thing from the LDF by the name of Ástor Moreau called my trusty manager and handler, Lou Savin, who I'd hired years ago to be my unbreachable stonewall to intrusions upon my valuable time. But Lou said the kid's voice was "sweet as honey" and couldn't bring himself to break the bad news in a good way, so he got me on the line with her for me to do his dirty work. Lou was right. Ástor was the princess of sweet-talk, and had an accent to die for that went with it.

The LDF, she told me, was on the cusp of a breakthrough in a vaccine cocktail that would stop the rampaging Lysen's Disease pandemic in its tracks. That caught my attention because my shows in Johannesburg had just been cancelled because of it and I was out six figures, big time. LDF was offering to fly me down to its research facility on the island of Lesser Nolena, "a tiny emerald jewel surrounded by the clear turquoise of the Caribbean." The reason? To entertain at a gala midnight dinner where the LDF would celebrate the success of their $500 million campaign to provide the means to mass-produce and distribute the vaccine.

"We can't imagine anyone in the world more than you who would attract the kind of people we've needed to raise this kind of money," she said. She probably thought such flattery would have me eating out of the palm of her hand. And she would be right. So did her offer for me to name my price.

"Continue," I said.

The tests were still in the experimental stage, Ástor went on, but with the pledges they'd already received from this august gathering they were confident it would get them over the hump. Every moment was precious. Between two and three thousand sub-Saharan Africans a day—a day!— were dying an excruciating death from the inside out. Lysen's Disease, named after Harding Lysen, the physician who first diagnosed it in Sierra Leone and then succumbed to it shortly thereafter, is an equal opportunity killer; a virus that strikes young and old, sick or healthy, with such astonishing and lethal virulence that it has universally been nicknamed Shark Flu. Symptoms begin with a mild fever, then dryness of the throat, followed by vomiting, diarrhea, convulsions, internal bleeding, external bleeding through all the orifices including the eyes, and then death. All within three to four days. "And I'm sparing you the nasty parts," Ástor said. The survival rate was zero. Shark Flu was barreling toward North Africa and was threatening to hop the Atlantic to the Caribbean. If it wasn't stopped, it was forecast to reach the shores of North America and Europe within weeks. Nothing to this point, including quarantines and strict international immigration controls, had been able to even slow its progress. The thought that there was an imminent breakthrough was breathtaking.

"We're so close to achieving our goal," Ástor concluded. "At least, we think so," with emphasis on the "we." "What do you say?"

"Are you French?"

"Why do you ask?"

"Your accent. Your name. And I have an attraction for French women."

She laughed, musical as a right-hand arpeggio.

"No. I am not French. I was born and raised in Trinidad."

"Will you be there?" I asked.

"Where. In Trinidad?" I think she was teasing me. The coy thing.

"I mean in Little Norena, or whatever it's called."

"Of course. It was my idea to invite you."

Around Ástor's little finger I was wrapped. I even declined to accept a fee.

Getting to the more appealing islands in the Caribbean is never a comfortable schlep. Maybe that's why they're still appealing. Fewer tourists. Getting to Lesser Nolena, an easily overlooked dot on the map, was a pain in the rear. And for some reason this whole business was suddenly hush-hush as an FBI investigation. Immediately after saying bye-bye to Ástor, I received a follow-up call from the big man himself, Dr. Liam MacDowell, Nobel laureate and the head researcher of LDF. He thanked me profusely for agreeing to lend my talents, after which he surprised me by insisting I not divulge anything about the event to anyone, even to Lou. I balked at that, but he impressed upon me how delicate a situation this was, with so many people dying every day and not wanting to get anyone's hopes up prematurely. And since, like all the other guests, I could plan to return home the next day, I would hardly be missed. It was probable no one would even know I had been gone.

I asked MacDowell how they expected the bigwigs to come to the island if no one knew about it, which I immediately realized was a dumb question. This was clearly an invitation only event. On the other hand, I would've thought an imminent breakthrough like this should have been advertised on all the front pages, especially since all the news we'd been hearing about Shark Flu was bad. MacDowell politely but firmly demurred, saying that science, not promotion, was his field. He left that to the president of the LDF, Art Henderson. Marketing is definitely not my thing, either, but knowing the little you hear about dueling pharmaceutical companies on the news, I suspected the main reason for secrecy was LDF's desire to keep their billion-dollar patent close to the vest. So I agreed to MacDowell's request, and when I phoned Lou I fabricated some malarkey about having to get away for a day for R and R. You know, the strain of the job. That kind of thing. I could picture him raising his eyebrows over the phone, but he wouldn't make a fuss.

I left Miami at about nine-thirty p.m. in an eight-seat prop-jet for Greater Nolena, a hop, skip, and jump from Florida, but which, the pilot informed me, is as close as one can get by plane to our final destination. When we landed I was pointed in the direction of the marina, all of a ten-minute walk from the runway. At the dock I was whisked onto a private yacht named Therapy II, handed a martini, and was splashily introduced (no pun intended) to a couple dozen high roller dinner guests who had been awaiting my arrival. As we skimmed over several miles of dark, open sea to the tiny, newly developed harbor at Lesser Nolena— which until the research facility was built had been inhabited only by parrots and geckos— we exchanged meaningless small talk animated by the import of the event and sounding, I would guess, like parrots. I have no idea what kind of noises a gecko makes.

At the Lesser Nolena dock we were greeted deferentially by LDF staff, who escorted us to barely comfortable accommodations. Clearly constructed in haste for our brief stay, you could still smell the fresh, lime green paint. Our bedrooms were in a plain, one story rectangular building that had more of a feel of a dormitory than a hotel. My room was furnished with a twin bed on a metal Harvard frame, which I hadn't seen since my college days—which maybe explains why I dropped out—a mirror, a portable clothing rack, and a no-frills bathroom. I suspected all the rooms were more or less the same. It certainly wasn't conducive to my fantasies of romancing the fair Ástor. What puzzled me, though, was that most of the guests were extremely busy Fortune 500 execs. If they had known they were going to be treated to such Spartan conditions, they might have chosen not to spend the night, or not have come at all—they could have just sent in their checks—but for the persuasiveness of the Foundation administrators that this was going to be a unique historic event. The LDF also hadn't hesitated to drop my name as the headline attraction, which was okay with me. But I mean, why bother with any of this?

It's no secret I am not unaccustomed to late night activity. My show in Vegas alone doesn't end until the wee hours, and that's when the party gets rolling. So doing a midnight gig did not ruffle my feathers. On the other hand, after being whisked across the Caribbean to Never Never Land and shown my Boy Scout accommodations, I was more than ready for a drink, for which, thankfully, I did not have long to wait. I changed from my travel clothes into a smart, $5,000 Savile Row black tuxedo. Nothing outlandish, like I would wear for the weekend slot addicts in Vegas. But appropriate for a serious occasion such as this one: saving the world. I knew, though, considering the company, that even decked out in my sartorial splendor I would not be a swan among a flock of ducks. I was struck how youthful all the guests seemed—some half my age—both male and female. The world has certainly changed from the days corporate magnates wore three-piece wool suits, carried pocket watches, and sported walrus mustaches. Now they looked like tennis pros and Sports Illustrated swimsuit models, and the high tech billionaires looked like teenagers. Maybe they were.

The order of ceremonies was going to be pretty standard: happy hour, hors d'oeuvres, a welcome from the LDF president, a sit-down dinner on the veranda, my command performance, and then the spiel by Dr. MacDowell, who would talk about their scientific breakthrough and thank us for our participation and support. And after that? The night was young. My kinky imagination took wing.

And so the "evening" proceeded in the manner of well-planned fundraisers, with the momentum gradually building up to the big announcement. Cocktail hour commenced under a starry sky, little waves lapping on the shore mere steps from the wet bar. The bartender and servers were all big guys whose white tuxedos were stretched tight over their biceps. My experienced eye tagged them as bouncers more than waiters, but this whole scenario was already so out of the ordinary I chose not to dwell on that.

There was a gentle tap on my shoulder. I turned to face a man wearing bifocals who seemed about my age—mid-fifties—with a trimmed salt-and-pepper beard, inside of which was a smile that might normally be genuine but which seemed, on this occasion, an attempt to disguise an overriding unease.

"Dr. MacDowell, I presume," I said.

"How did you know?" he asked, the smile brightening momentarily.

"Seen too many sci fi movies on Netflix."

We shook hands and he once again expressed his gratitude for my blah blah blah. The usual spiel. But it was nice. Don't believe what anyone tells you. It never gets old.

MacDowell was clearly preoccupied with the purpose of the evening, so I quickly released him to whatever schmoozing he was obligated to do.

One of the servers passed with a silver tray of bubbly. I grabbed two flutes of champagne and asked him to point out Ástor Moreau. Right where the water ended and the sand began I was rewarded with a vision of paradise. Miss Moreau, maybe thirty, maybe less. Bronzed skin the result of serious sunbathing or an intriguing racial mix. Either way, I liked it. Light brown eyes and shoulder-length auburn hair and the profile of a goddess. And did I mention her figure?

"Enjoying the evening, Ástor?"

"Ah! I am so glad you came to our little soirée," she said, holding out her hand. Since I had a flute in each hand, I couldn't shake it, so I handed her a glass, accompanied by my winningest smile, and gave her a peck on the cheek. Both cheeks. We clinked glasses.

"Delighted to be here," I said.

"I've arranged for you to sit next to me at the table of honor."

"I'm honored."

"So then you won't mind being my guinea pig for the evening?" she said, with what appeared to be mock seriousness. Or was it a Mona Lisa smile?

It was a strange way of putting things, "guinea pig," but no stranger than anything else that had taken place on this island. And what is it they say about gift horses? Not that Ástor's mouth wasn't something one could look at for hours on end. Ah, the potential!

"I've been waiting my whole life for an invitation like that," I said, and we both laughed.

With such a compressed itinerary, by the time cocktail hour was over everyone was buddy-buddy, and with the research team conspicuously absent the island vibe felt more Club Med than medical. And that's how it sounded when we were welcomed by the president of the Lysen's Disease Foundation, Art Henderson. He told us all about how well things were going with their fund-raising efforts. What an honor it was to be surrounded by such a distinguished gathering of the rich and famous. In so many words he told us to eat, drink, and be merry. I'm glad he didn't get around to the end part, "for tomorrow we die." That would have put a real damper on the evening.

For dinner, the guests were seated at round tables with white linen tablecloths. Each table seated six, and had a centerpiece of local flowers. Nice touch. Chinese lanterns hung from the veranda's rafters. That was nice, too. At one of end of the veranda was the Steinway piano that had been flown in for the occasion, and thankfully seemed to still be intact. I told them to lose the candelabra. I'm not Liberace. No way.

The menu was highlighted by fresh, perfectly grilled shrimp and swordfish that had arrived from Greater Nolena in the same yacht as the guests. There was a lot of small talk, as if to sidestep discussing the reason we were there. Maybe it was because here we were, being wined and dined in the lap of luxury, just to get us to cough up money to put a stop to the ugliest form of human misery the world had ever known. Maybe it was because the guests felt vulnerable, that even all their money might not be able to save them. Was it excitement in the air? Or was there a hint of desperation?

Every seat on the veranda was taken except the one to my right. That was lucky for me because it enabled me to concentrate on making hay with my partner to my left, Ástor. I had a feeling this was going to be a night to remember. Toward the end of the meal, a musclebound server came up to me and whispered in my ear that it was time for me to perform. I thanked him for the heads-up and excused myself from the other four at my table.

"By the way," I asked Ástor, close to her ear, "who's the person that was supposed to sit next to me?"

"Oh, Liam MacDowell. He's my husband."

One may or may not like my style of music. To each, his own. But no one can ever say that I'm not a professional. I've dealt with more than my share of drunks, deviants, and power outages over the years, so putting Ástor's bombshell out of my mind for the next half hour while I did my thing was all in the line of duty. Not saying it was easy.

My performance of well-known but not too highbrow classics and Andrew Lloyd Webber hits created the desired heart-tugging, feel-good effect. I took requests from the audience for fan favorites from Les Miz, Rent, Wicked, and Hamilton, and was able to toss off every one of them as easily as flipping burgers. At the end I put in a good word for "my dear friends" at LDF, who I had met an hour before. By the time I returned to my seat next to Ástor and MacDowell took the podium, I'd primed the gathering to exceed the $500 million goal. One would have thought MacDowell would have been ebullient. He was anything but.

"I would like to thank all of you from the bottom of my heart for coming here tonight," he said, with a tone more funereal than celebratory.

"As you know, Lysen's Disease—Shark Flu—has been the most virulent communicable disease in history. It makes AIDS, Ebola, Zika, or the Black Death seem like a head cold."

A few people chuckled. MacDowell didn't even smile.

"It is a disease," he continued, "which, unless it is stopped, has the theoretical capacity to eradicate the entire population of the world—"

No laughs now.

"Which is why we have been working feverishly to develop a vaccine. Because Lysen's disease is incurable and untreatable, prevention is the only possibility. Let me repeat, we having been working feverishly to develop a vaccine because Lysen's disease is incurable and untreatable. Prevention is the only possibility."

He had the group's attention like a boa constrictor wrapped around a rabbit.

"One of the many challenges to effectively combat this disease is that, unlike any other virus we have ever encountered, Lysen's Disease attacks only humans and no other organism. Therefore, the testing we've done on flies, mice, rats, pigs, and even lower primates has been an exercise in futility. Regardless of the similarity of genetic predisposition, those subjects simply do not contract the disease, so inoculating them with the vaccine neither proves nor disproves anything."

A hand shot up. MacDowell waved it off dismissively.

"What we have tried to do here on Lesser Nolena is understand the nature of the viral organism itself, study how and why it has attached itself only to human tissue, and extrapolate from there, basing our strategy on how viruses we do understand have responded in the past. The serum we have concocted, we strongly believe—I repeat—we strongly believe will be successful in stopping the spread of the virus. But there is only one way to know."

The gathering of the powerful collectively leaned forward in their seats, waiting for the dénouement that would justify the donation of their time and their treasure.

"Ladies and gentlemen, we have brought you here today for two reasons. The first is to thank you for your commitment to humanity, for demonstrating your faith in our efforts by providing the financial means to literally save the world."

"Hear! Hear!" someone called out. Glasses were raised by all.

Out of the corner of my eye, I noticed the waiters in their white tuxedos set a discreet perimeter around the veranda, the kind of thing I'm used to seeing security guards do at the casinos on the Strip when the weirdos get out of hand. What's this all about? I asked myself. This is supposed to be a celebration.

"The second is again to thank you for your commitment to humanity, but for a different reason than you can ever have imagined. Look around you. You have probably noticed how young everyone is. But it is not your youth why you were selected to be on our guest list. Rather, it is because we've determined you have no committed partners or children. We are trying to be as humane as possible."

"What are you getting at, Dr. MacDowell?" someone shouted out. "Is this some kind of game?"

The guy's challenge was making everyone nervous, me included.

"As I've implied by my previous comments, we have had to break every rule in the book. The only way to know if our vaccine will work is to test it on humans. There was no time for double-blind testing. There was no time for peer review, patents, or FDA approval."

"You're going to give us shots?" someone yelled.

"That's unethical," someone else chimed in. "You can't do this, MacDowell!"

The crowd was stirring, but not in a happy way. It looked like things might get ugly, fast.

"We already have, sir." MacDowell was speaking loudly now, as the guests' commotion started to become unruly. One of the men tried to make a dash for it. Where "it" was was anyone's guess. But he was subdued in short order by one of the heavies, a real pro, and carried away like a sack of potatoes, presumably to his room.

"Ladies and gentlemen, your pre-dinner cocktails contained an oral dose of our vaccine. The delicious fish you enjoyed for dinner was injected with diluted Lysen's virus itself. We pray that we are correct and that tomorrow we will all witness a glorious sunrise over the Caribbean. If not," MacDowell said, raising his glass, "together we leave this world with good food and beautiful music." MacDowell motioned his glass in my direction, and gave me what could be construed as a wan smile. "May God bless you all."

"We're out of here, MacDowell!" someone else demanded. "We're leaving now and you can't stop us." The guy jumped up like a jack-in-the-box and overturned his table, sending the flowers, glassware and everything else shattering onto the floor.

"Stop you? I'm sorry to say, there is no way off the island. There are no boats, no planes, and all communications have been shut down until we have a result. We are all here until we know for certain. Surely you can understand that we can't let anyone go back if there is any chance of carrying this disease. But I assure you, we are confident of a positive result. A result that will save humanity."

Some of the guests were crying, and not just the women. Others sat immobilized, stone-faced as Easter Island statues. As reality set in, the fight seemed to have left everyone. There was either hope or there was hopeless. Whichever, there was nothing more to be done.

"I'm going to my room," someone said. "Wake me up when this nightmare is over."

That ended it. There were a few more mumbles about calling lawyers or "the government," but the insurrection ebbed as meekly as last call at a corner bar.

"Come," Ástor whispered to me.

We slid unnoticed past the numbed guests and stepped off the veranda. Ástor slipped off her shoes and we walked on night-chilled sand toward the water. The dark sea and moonless sky, which had so recently seemed so enchanting, so beckoning, so full of potential, now seemed so empty. We were a speck on a black world and in a matter of hours either there would be a new day, or there would be...nothing.

I looked at Ástor.

"Now I know what you meant by guinea pig," I said.

"I'm sorry. I couldn't tell you. I wasn't allowed."

"He's either a genius or a madman, your husband. Which is it?"

"I wish I knew."

"So what do we do now?" I asked. "Just wait?"

She looked into my eyes and gave me that Mona Lisa smile again.

"What would you recommend? Watching the sun rise?"

Gerald Elias, author of the Daniel Jacobus mystery series and many other publications, is a former violinist with the Boston Symphony and Utah Symphony orchestras. geraldeliasmanofmystery.wordpress.com
(Last Night, *written a few years ago, is reprinted from Elias's collection,* "...an eclectic anthology of 28 short mysteries to chill the warmest heart.")

A Light Touch
by Katherine Fast

"I'm here for Community Service," Kathy Moore says to the receptionist of the Wellington Nursing Home who is brushing polish along a long nail.

The woman—Judy according to the nameplate—doesn't look up. She elbows the paper aside, protecting her wet nails and her bottle of Rhapsody Red polish. "Sit," she orders, nodding toward a row of wooden straight-backed chairs against the wall. She continues to paint the fingers of her left hand.

Kathy shuffles to a chair and plops down. The heavy scent of disinfectant barely disguises a strong undercurrent of urine. *Breathe through your mouth.* She watches Judy surreptitiously from the side of the room. Nails are definitely the woman's best feature. Her delicate fingers are attached to pudgy hands, mammoth arms, and a frightening torso crammed into a stretchy top that accentuates roll after roll of middle-aged flab.

Bet she has teensy little feet to match. Pancake makeup on the woman's face doesn't quite reach her scalp of thinning hair. A slash of violent red lipstick duplicates the woman's polish. Kathy reminds herself that not all fat, obnoxious people are stupid, and to be on her guard.

"Another naughty one." Judy switches the brush to her right hand. "So what did you do to earn the privilege of service here?"

Kathy doesn't bother to respond. She'd spend her afternoons here for the next week because she'd been caught shoplifting a stupid magazine.

She studies the forlorn surroundings—faded rose wallpaper, curled linoleum, and stained industrial carpet. Two old ladies watch her from wheelchairs across the room. What a way to end up, stuffed in here. One woman farts and the other giggles.

Judy polishes her pinkie and blows on her nails. "Not so talkative are we?" She glances at the paper. "Shoplifting, eh? I'll assign you to Florence. Whatever junk you tried to steal isn't worth a week of visits with Flo." She chuckles. "She's got an attitude like yours. You'll get along great."

Behind Judy's desk to the left, an open door labeled Assisted Living leads down a long corridor. On the right, a sign on a closed door reads, Medical Staff Only.

Judy greets workers as the shift changes. She presses a buzzer on back of her desk to electronically unlock the door to Medical, allowing a nurse to enter.

Kathy thumbs through messages on her phone.

"Steal that phone?" baits Judy.

Kathy types a reply.

"No cellphones allowed inside. Leave it with me."

Not on your life. Kathy tucks the phone into her backpack.

Finally, Judy presses another button on her console and announces via intercom for the whole place to hear, "This month's little helper is here. Another budding young felon. Petty larceny. Hide your wallets." She shakes a bottle of topcoat and addresses Kathy. "Afraid you've come to the wrong place. Anything worth stealing was cleaned out long ago."

An attendant returns from her cigarette break. "This one's for Florence," Judy announces as a matter of introduction. She and the attendant exchange knowing smirks. Judy stretches her hands before her to examine her artwork. "She's all yours."

The attendant beckons for Kathy to follow her down the hall. "Flo don't talk much, but she can, don't let her fool you none." She opens a door. "In here."

Kathy follows her into a small room. A shriveled old woman is propped up with pillows in a bed that takes up half the room. She's a solid wrinkle with two indentations for eyes. Looks like one of those hideous hairless cats.

"Florence, meet your newest helper, Kathy."

Florence's head slowly turns and her eyes fix Kathy with stare. Her hand topples a glass from a tray next to the bed. It rolls off the cart and spills liquid onto the floor.

"A little grumpy today, are we?" The attendant turns to Kathy. "That's why everything's plastic here."

Flo reaches over and pushes her lunch tray off the cart and returns her gaze to the soundless, flickering image on the TV mounted above the bed.

"She's on strike because she don't like the lunch. She gets the same one every day. Because of the ink. Only get one copy of the menu per room a week and her last helper filled in the choices in ink. Clean up this mess, and then I'll show you how to change the bedpan. Mops and stuff are in the closet at the end of the hall." The attendant turns to Flo. "Use pencil." She snatches a paper and pencil from the bureau and places them on the bed. She leaves without another word of instruction.

Kathy glares at the old crone in the bed. Waste of space. Why keep these old fossils around? They don't do anything. Make anything. Serve any useful purpose. Just a drain on everyone else's time and money. And they stink.

Must be eighty degrees. Kathy is dressed in teenage camouflage, a navy hoodie, faded jeans with shredded knees, and sneakers with no socks. Her hoodie is stuck to her back. She'd remove it, but doesn't have anything underneath. She walks to the window and moves aside a sad little plant. She ignores the Do Not Open sign and shoves up the window.

She gets a broom and mop from the closet. The glob of food on the floor has a ghastly institutional greenish hue. " *Yew.* I'd dump this crap, too." She collects it with paper towels, washes the floor, and returns the equipment.

Back in the room, she watches Flo grip the menu in claw fingers, and draw it to within an inch of her face. She grunts in frustration and tosses it to the floor.

The old bat can't see to read the menu. Kathy picks up the menu and pencil. Great, the lead is broken. She fishes about for a pencil in her pack but can only find a pen. "If I fill this out, you promise not to dump your tray tomorrow?" Flo nods.

"They have broccoli." Flo shakes her head. "Carrots?" Flo's head bobs and Kathy checks off the item. "Tomorrow you have a choice of spaghetti or tuna casserole. Spaghetti, right?" The rest of the afternoon is uneventful except for mind-numbing television and then the disgusting task of emptying the bedpan and cleaning up Flo.

The next day, the attendant scolds Kathy for filling out the lunch menu in ink. "I told you to use pencil. We erase and recycle here. She'll be having carrots and spaghetti for the rest of the week."

Kathy holds up the pencil with the broken lead.

"Looks like you got a problem. I can't do everything around here."

Kathy makes a rude gesture at the back of the attendant as she leaves the room and is surprised to catch a sly wrinkle of a smile on Flo's face.

Kathy waits for Judy to waddle past the room toward the lunchroom on her break. She checks to make sure no one is in the hall, and sneaks back to Reception. It takes but a second to palm a small bottle of correction fluid and slip back down the hall to Flo's room. She whites out the inked in selections on the menu and then stealthily returns the bottle to Judy's desk.

When she gets back, she picks up the worthless pencil. She fishes around in her pockets and withdraws a metal cylinder. When she presses a button on the side, a blade snaps out. Flo gasps and her eyes fix on the deadly blade. Kathy grins and whittles the end of the pencil to a fine point, re-folds the knife and returns it to her pocket.

Together, she and Flo fill in the next day's selections.

Two days later, Kathy enters with a pair of magnifiers. She removes the sticker from the side of the glasses and hands them to Flo.

"Where did..." Flo stops mid-sentence when Kathy shakes her head. "Don't you go getting into trouble on my account. I won't be here long. You've got a whole life to go."

Kathy just shrugs. She wanders about the room. Slim pickins indeed. She asks herself, if you die a near-vegetable in a lousy nursing home all alone, could you possibly have had a good life? Is there any dignity in old age? Or just unending days of pain and loneliness? For that matter, if you end up working at a dump like this nursing home, you can't be where you want to be either. What a lousy job.

Afternoons go on forever. Boooooooring. Trash TV. She can't use her phone. Toward the end of her week, Kathy paces around while Flo does what she does best, snoring and snuffling the rest of her life away. Quietly Kathy explores the far side of the room. A small bookcase with a few novels and what looks like a scrapbook. A bureau. She opens the drawers one at a time. Underwear and nighties and an old sweater. Good lord, is this all she has?

A small box atop the bureau looks more promising. She shields her hands from view in case Flo awakens, and opens the lid. A jewelry box! She pokes around inside. Nothing but trashy, costume jewelry. She picks up a shiny earring. Glass and a clip-on. Judy was right. There's nothing left to steal. Anything of value was long since harvested.

"You'll never make it as a thief."

Kathy whirls about, knocking the cheap jewelry box to the floor, and is face to face with the attendant who has crowded up directly behind her. The attendant smirks. "The earring might look cute on you. Pick up those things."

Kathy turns and her eyes meet Flo's. The old fossil stares at her as if she's a bug. Did she see her snooping? Did she press the emergency button to call for help? Kathy can't tell. Flo closes her eyes and rolls to the side.

As Kathy bends over and collects the box and scattered jewelry, something glints in the light catching her eye. She touches it. A slender chain. She quickly slips it into her pocket and continues to gather the other pieces.

"Time for toenails."

Kathy takes the toenail clippers from the attendant.

"Help me get her into the wheelchair and then fill that pan with warm, soapy water." They struggle to get Flo into a wheelchair, but she acts as a dead weight to make it hard for them. "She does this every time. I'm warning you, this is not her favorite thing." Finally they strap her upright and Kathy fetches water for soaking.

Kathy kneels and lifts away the edges of Flo's nightgown. She backs away suddenly at the sight of flaky, scaly skin and random, silky hairs, remnants of times past. The veins on the spindly legs are so close to the surface of the paper-thin skin that they give the legs a bluish tint. Long, yellowed nails and overgrown cuticles look like they belong to a raptor. Kathy lifts each leg gingerly and places it in the pan.

"You'll have to soak 'em for a while. Good luck," laughs the attendant on her way out the door.

The second she's out of sight, Flo kicks her feet forward, splashing water all over Kathy. Instinctively, Kathy splashes back, soaking Flo's legs. Flo paddles furiously, dousing Kathy as best she can. The battle rages until both are dripping wet and laughing.

"What's going on here?" The attendant pops her head in and surveys the mess. She shakes her head and scowls at Kathy. "Get the mop. Now you'll need to change her nightie before you do the nails." It's as if the attendants and nurses were waiting right outside the door. Kathy is this month's entertainment, the most exciting thing that's happened since their last helper. They're just waiting for her to mess up.

Kathy struggles to remove and change Flo's nightie while she's sitting in the chair, Eventually she prevails. The second time she puts Flo's feet in water, Flo cooperates. After fifteen minutes, Kathy kneels again and opens the nail clippers. She holds them up and looks into Flo's eyes. "Truce?" Flo nods.

"Jesus, these things are weapons!" Kathy exclaims, struggling to close the clippers on the talon of Flo's big toe.

The attendant returns and kicks a scrofulous pair of thin and faded slippers toward Kathy. They're old, all pilled up and smelly. "When you're finished, put these on her."

"Have any gloves?" Kathy mumbles under her breath.

"I heard that. We don't need a smart mouth around here. "

Kathy glares at the attendant for a long moment but holds her tongue. *Only a week*, she tells herself. *Don't invite a bad report.*

The toenails take over an hour. When she's finished Kathy empties the water in the bathroom and takes a moment to examine her prize. She withdraws the chain from her pocket.

Omigod. It looks like gold! Delicate double strands of chain are linked every two inches by two circle rings. What a find! Kathy had never owned anything like it. The clasp was so small, it was hard to fasten behind her neck. Flo's gnarly fingers would never be able to manage it. She'd never wear it again. And somehow the nurses and attendants had missed it.

Did Flo know it was still there? She had no way to get to the box, and given the dust that had been on the cover, it hadn't been touched for a long time. Kathy admires the necklace in the mirror before tucking it under the neck of her hoodie and leaving the bathroom.

"Oh no you don't. We're on to you."

Kathy's hand flies to her neck. Busted!

"Empty your pockets."

"Oh. Right." With a sheepish smile Kathy dumps the nail clippers onto the desk.

"I'd report you, but it's too much paperwork."

"Sorry. I just forgot. In all the excitement. You saw. Flo fought back."

"Sure. Watch yourself, girlie."

The next afternoon she empties the bedpan when they take Flo to physical therapy. What's the use? They can wave her arms and legs around, but Flo's not going to get any better. Why extend a pathetic life? She's miserable. No smiles. No relief. No hope. No visitors. Just waiting for it to be over.

Time for a little excitement. When Flo returns and is re-propped on the bed, Kathy places the Emergency Call button in her hands and then stands behind the door with her back to the wall. She raises her hand, puts her forefinger to her lips, and then mimes pressing the button. She has to do it twice before Flo understands and hits the button.

They wait. They wait longer. So much for emergency service. Five minutes pass. Kathy checks her watch and signals for Flo to hit it again. Finally they hear the nurse walking down the hall.

The nurse enters. "What do you want?"

Kathy clears her throat directly behind her. The nurse jumps and drops her clipboard. "What the hell are you trying to pull?"

Kathy shrugs and looks at her watch. "Took you long enough," she comments.

"We like to give them time to shuffle off."

Kathy can't believe her ears.

"What's your problem?" The nurse addresses Flo.

Flo moans and holds her tummy.

"Good grief. Constipated again?" The nurse shakes her head and withdraws a bottle from her pocket. She shakes out a pill. "Get her some water." She places the pill in Flo's hand and stomps out.

Flo wrinkles her nose at the attendant's back. "Cow." Amazing how Flo can rearrange the grooves in her skin to make such a naughty face.

Her eyes glint with mischief. She uncurls her fingers. The pill rests in her palm. A quick flick of her fingers and the pill sails across the room.

Kathy laughs and signals a thumbs up.

Nothing to do. Nothing. Kathy wanders to the bookcase and picks up the scrapbook. Flo nods encouragement. Kathy takes the book to the bed, props herself up beside Flo, and opens up the record of the old woman's life. With the reading glasses, Flo can see images in her scrapbook.

Flo's wrinkles form a genuine smile. The first pictures in black and white are serious poses and family shots. Flo points a gnarled claw at one of the girls in a baby photo and then points to herself. As they turn the pages, Flo grows into a gangly teenager and then high school student where the pictures change to color. A beautiful young woman wearing a prom dresses with crinolines beams on the arm of a tall, handsome young man. A dance card, filled in with the names of male dance partners, is pasted into the book. Kathy wonders if any of them are still alive.

When they get to wedding photos, Flo whispers, "Vernon." What a handsome couple. Kathy looks closely at a more detailed portrait of Flo as a bride and sees the delicate gold chain circling her neck. She glances at Flo who is beaming, her eyes brimming with tears.

Kathy debates with herself all the way home. Flo will never wear the necklace again. She doesn't even know it's missing. So what, it doesn't belong to you. It's the only thing of value, the only thing the old woman could care about that's left in her pitiful, little room. But it's so lovely. I earned it emptying bedpans, cutting toenails, and entertaining the old girl.

But argue as she will, Kathy can't erase the image of younger, radiant bride, Flo, wearing the necklace.

The next afternoon she battles with her conscience all the way to the nursing home. After lunch, she ducks into the bathroom and unclasps the necklace. When she reenters the room she walks to the jewelry box, opens a drawer and pretends to rummage around. She looks over her shoulder to make sure Flo is watching.

"Wow! Look at this!" Kathy exclaims. She carries the little necklace to Flo.

Flo gasps in surprise and her eyes light up. She grips the chain in her hand like a long-lost treasure.

"Would you like to wear it?" Kathy asks.

Flo smiles, yes. Very gently, Kathy closes the clasp around Flo's neck.

"Beautiful," Kathy sighs.

Flo touches the chain, her face wreathed in a radiant smile.

"What're you doing here? Your week's up." Judy daubs her fingers with a cotton ball soaked in stinky nail polish remover.

Kathy ignores her and walks to the door for Assisted Living.

"What's in the bag?" Judy challenges.

"Slippers." Kathy stops and withdraws soft pink slippers in a plastic wrapper from her backpack.

"Where'd you steal those from?"

"Macy's," Kathy walks toward Flo's room.

"Well, you're too late," Judy calls after her.

Flo's door is closed. Kathy opens it. The room is completely bare. The empty bed has been stripped of sheets. No scrapbook. No little jewelry box. The closet is empty. Everything is wiped clean. Window latched, shade drawn, plant gone. It's as if Flo had never been there.

The nurse follows her into the room. "Flo had a turn for the worse. She's been moved to Medical."

Kathy's shoulders slump and a lump forms in her throat. "Thanks," she mumbles as she backs to the door and rushes back down the hall to Reception. She notices Flo's little plant on the desk. Judy follows her eyes. "Someone has to water it."

"I'd like to see her."

"No visitors in Medical," Judy points to the sign.

"Just to say, goodbye. I won't stay."

"Them's the rules," Judy shakes her head.

In one swift motion, Kathy throws the slippers on the desk to distract Judy, rushes behind the desk and mashes the button that releases the lock. She's through the door to Medical before Judy can lift her fat ass from the chair. "You can't go in there!"

Kathy runs down the hall, searching one room after another, finding bodies in every bed, but no Florence.

Judy waddles after her. "Stop her!"

At the end of the hall she finally finds Flo's room and enters. Flo is no longer propped up. She's lying flat on her back, eyes closed, connected to machines by tubes. Kathy draws up a chair, sits and reaches for Flo's hand. It's hard to tell if she's still breathing. "Hi, Flo. It's Kathy." She thinks she sees Flo's eyelids flutter in response, but can't be sure.

She looks closer. The delicate necklace is gone. What had she expected? She looks to Flo's left hand. The gold band is still on her ring finger. Small victory. They couldn't force it over her arthritic knuckle. Kathy closes her eyes and sits with the old lady in silence.

An hour later, the nurse enters and says, "Time to go, honey. Best say good-bye. She won't wake again."

Kathy leans over and kisses Flo on the forehead. The nurse and receptionist watch her from the doorway. She pushes past them, head down, unexpected tears streaming down her cheeks. She pauses at Reception for a moment, kicks the desk and picks up the slippers and backpack she'd left there.

Two days later, her mother enters Kathy's bedroom wearing a pair of new soft pink slippers. "Mail for you." She places an envelope on a table next to Kathy.

Kathy's name appears on the first line in a shaky, tortured script. Below the name, someone else had written in the street address.

Kathy pushes the envelope aside and makes a production of painting her nails with bright red polish. Her mother waits, dying of curiosity. Kathy never gets mail.

"Like the color?" Kathy holds up the bottle of Rhapsody Red polish. "When I'm done, I'll do your toenails if you like."

"Well, are you going to open it?"

Kathy holds up her hand and blows on her nails. "Have to wait for my nails to dry." She waits until her mother leaves before tearing open the envelope. Empty. *Huh.*

She shakes it.

Out falls a delicate gold necklace.

Katherine Fast lives in Massachusetts with her husband, German Shepherd and three cats. She enjoys writing stories, dabbling in watercolor, and red wine.

A Silver Lining
by Priscilla Halberg

If ever there was a time to err on the side of caution, this was it. Worried about viral pathways into my lungs from post-nasal drip, I gargled with hot salt water every night, and dosed with elderberry syrup as a tonic and immune builder. Not everyone was being as conscientious. Pictures of mass graves in Iran and obituaries in Italy flooded newspapers and social media. Coronavirus, a world-wide pandemic, is a terrible thing. Could the whole world unify by fighting something other than each other? I hoped so.

I didn't want to think too much about the claim it might not have happened naturally. That there were facilities in Wuhan, China where biological warfare research was conducted. And that the source of the original health crisis, where the disease spread from a single individual to close to 50,000 people almost overnight, was Wuhan.

There had been criticism of the Chinese Wild Animal Wet Market in Wuhan, where people bought food not grown or raised on a farm. Someone suggested that people eating bats was the origin of the pandemic, because bats carried corona virus. I saw a photo of a woman eating a bat, with chopsticks! Bizarre, but then again I'm not an adventurous eater. The caption under the photo said that not only Coronavirus, but SARS (Severe Acute Respiratory Syndrome) may have come from eating bats. I've traveled around Asia, and as a patient of practitioners of traditional Chinese medicine, or TCM, I'd learned that the ingredients of some of their medicinal teas included wild animals. I try not to judge. There are certainly lots of other people with unusual diets. The Explorer's Club, an American multidisciplinary professional society promoting scientific exploration and field study, holds a dinner once a year in New York. What they eat at that dinner makes the Chinese Wild Animal Wet Market fare look relatively tame. Things like Madagascar cockroaches! They must dare each other: "Bet you can't eat just one!" A thought flashed through my head: You are what you eat?

There was hardly anyone on the streets, and I encountered only a few brave neighbors on my daily walk down by the river. In normal times we'd often stopped to chat. This morning my neighbor, Don, let me pet his dog, Grace, a big friendly smooth collie. Before the pandemic, Don had always been a little standoffish, holding his dog back. Today, as much as I appreciated Don's congeniality, I tried to maintain social distancing, even with Grace. It was certainly an adjustment getting used to the new restrictions.

So, what is everyone doing for exercise? The gyms are all closed. Treadmills and stationary bikes in their homes? I'd signed up for Aquatic Aerobics. I made it to two classes and loved it, exertion and relaxation at the same time. But then they cancelled the class, at least for the rest of the month. I'll miss visiting with the people there, too. Of course, with restaurants closed I'm cooking at home. And beginning to enjoy it! I've shed a few pounds, walk more, and my blood sugar is going down. Life is much simpler. A silver lining?

When I got home, I called my neighbor, Kathy, a senior citizen. "Do you need someone to help you walk the dog?" I asked. Why not? It helps keep me calm, too.

"I'm all set with that," Kathy said, "but if you really want to help maybe you could pick up some alcohol wipes for me. For doorknobs and bathroom fixtures after my friends visit."

"Good idea," I said. "I'm teaching tomorrow. I'll pick some up for myself too."

I teach violin. Since the schools have been closed for a week, and will be for at least two more, music teachers are experimenting with Skype and Zoom. But I really enjoy spending time with the students and they didn't want to cancel their in-person lessons, so I decided to teach them at the recommended six-feet social distancing.

"How are you doing with school work at home?" I asked Mirabella, a fourteen-year-old eighth grader, when she arrived for her lesson.

"Okay," she said. "I'm not having trouble with the work, but it's so boring! I can't spend any time with my friends."

"Are you on Facebook?"

"Well, I'm not really allowed," Mirabella frowned.

I thought a bit and then made a suggestion.

"What if we plan on a virtual recital on Zoom, where you can invite friends to tune in to hear you? That would give you something to shoot for in your practice, and you can talk about it with your friends after."

Mirabella didn't have to think very long.

"Would you accompany me? I've never played a whole recital before."

"Happily," I said, and lavishly praised Mirabella's courage and willingness to try something new.

My younger students and I often make up words to the songs they're learning to help them memorize the music. The kids enjoy it and often come up with great lyrics on their own. For "Go Tell Aunt Rhody," my seven-year-old beginner, Jade, sang:

> *Go tell Aunt Rhody*
> *I want bugs for lunch.*
> *I'll have mosquitoes*
> *Flies and spiders too,*
> *I'll have mosquitoes*
> *Spiders too.*

And maybe Madagascar cockroaches?

With furrowed brow, Jade was beginning to learn bow distribution. It was challenging but she was being a trooper. Miguel, a fifth grader, was diligently learning to play *spiccato*. I felt good teaching these youngsters who suddenly had extra time to learn and practice, and an even greater need for self-discipline. At a time like this, little things take on a lot more significance and burn more brightly in the memory, even in a world where live concerts are suspended and virtual ones rule.

People seem to be pulling together. Paradoxically, even in a time of social distancing, the overall mood seems much more caring. Concern for the needy and a desire to help are becoming commonplace. People seem less competitive and more accepting. If only we could be like this without there having to be a pandemic.

Even my family has gotten closer. When I was young, my family was close—a large, brash, immigrant family keeping alive the customs from the "old country." Time changed all that. We had become all but estranged, except two years ago I held a hundredth birthday party—and then, sadly, a memorial service—for my mother, the last of her generation in the family. Now, everyone is reaching out. Relatives have started a group letter to keep in touch and offer support. Maybe when the pandemic is over, we'll remember this time and these new coping skills. I certainly hope so. It's a better world that way.

Much to my surprise, I've started to feel better through the quarantine. When all of my "team" of helpers—chiropractor, masseuse, acupuncturist, and physical therapist—closed up shop because of the lockdown, I wondered how I'd manage. But now, my various medical issues seem more bearable. Enforced confinement has given me a chance to rest up. Permission to take it easy. Get more rest. The stress is off. Nobody is expected to accomplish a lot during a pandemic. Is that at odds with all the concerns of the world? Could it be that simple? Probably not for everyone, though I wish it were so.

Priscilla Halberg, violinist, aspiring writer and a 27-year veteran of the Boston Pops-Esplanade Orchestra, lives in Albuquerque, where she is the Executive Director and Lead Teacher of the String Academy of the Southwest. https://www.stringacademyofthesouthwest.org/priscilla-hallberg

Birding in the Time of Corona
by John Harrison

Stepping into the woods as I usually do has been different lately. On a recent visit, I looked overhead and the Cooper's Hawk that I see so often in this part of the woods, close to its nest, soared overhead, looking down on the world below. It didn't know it was looking down on a somewhat different world. A world in the grips of the Coronavirus, COVID-19. This hawk was oblivious to that. Watching the hawk effortlessly soar was as exhilarating as always. And yet, with exhortations to "shelter in place" and "socially distance" and the daily briefings and the uncertainty, the exhilaration had a different feel. News reports on the spread of the virus that I watched before leaving for the woods were sent to the back of my mind. The sheer beauty of a raptor in flight would, you might think, be dimmed by what was happening in the world beyond the woods. Not so! As I walked, the leaves crunching below my shoes, the Corona reality whooshed out of me and the wonder of the birds and the forest took hold. This I could always count on. The power of nature and its flyers always took me out of this world. There were only the trees and that Cooper's Hawk soaring above. That's the wondrous power of nature and these things with feathers. They are magical.

I veered off of the main path into a section of the woods where the Coops, as these Cooper's Hawks are affectionately called, were building a nest. There was another Cooper's Hawk nest, maybe a three-minute walk from this second nest, where a Coop family had hatched chicks for several years. That I discovered this new nest activity was serendipity. A few days before, a male Coop flew over me with a branch in its beak. I followed its flight and it landed in a tree nearby. I walked closer to that tree and raised my binoculars. By God, I could see a nest! I saw that familiar activity that we always see in raptor nests. The hawk was moving that twig around, finding the perfect place for it. I saw its head pop into view now and then as it worked on the nest. Raptors, the big birds, are hard workers. Every day they devote time to nest-building as breeding time gets closer. They fly in and out of the nest with branches they pull off trees. I watched the nest and in a few minutes the hawk flew out and landed on a tree nearby and pulled off another twig and flew back to the nest. So interesting to watch. However, this begged a question. Would a new pair of Cooper's Hawks be building a nest in the territory of a pair that has held this turf for years? That's a challenge that would bring out the established pair on a war footing. They would chase this new pair out. No doubt about it. Raptors are territorial and guard their nest like the New England Patriots used to guard Tom Brady. (A story for another time.) So what was going on here? Nature and wildlife are so often full of mysteries and incongruities. As much as we know, there's as much that we don't know. Which is a good thing. There should always be some unknowns. As I ruminated on this mystery, the Coronavirus was out of mind. The natural world had my total attention.

I showed this second nest to a friend who spends hours in these woods each day and has done so for years. He explained that this new nest was an auxiliary. It wasn't a new pair challenging the resident pair. Of course, knowing exactly why they were building this auxiliary nest was a matter of conjecture. Were they going to use this nest next year? Or was this a just-in-case home if something happened to the old nest? Raptors do build second nests, so this could be explained in several ways. At least *some* of the mystery was no longer a mystery. I continued to watch the Coops fly around with the male bringing twigs to the nest while the female perched on trees in the area watching her mate shore up that nest.

Sometimes the female devoured prey while her mate continued the nest building. Once, while the female was eating a chipmunk, the male flew in and dropped down and they mated. And I was ready with my camera and caught the entire scene. OMG! I had photographed Red-tailed Hawks and Bald Eagles mating, but catching a pair of Coops mating was a surprise. Coops are not seen nearly as much as Red-tailed

Hawks or the nearby Bald Eagles we watch, so catching them mating was a treat. While the female continued eating her chipmunk after this mating sequence, the male flew off and pulled a twig and flew up to the nest with it. And a couple more times after that. About fifteen minutes later, as the female was still eating the prey, the male flew to that tree limb and they mated again. And I was ready again, camera aimed. Holy Moly! That beautiful pair, with their striking rust-speckled chests, looked right down at me as they united. Their fierce red eyes drilled into my consciousness. The force was with me. And for that time in the woods, and all times in the woods, there was no such thing as COVID-19.

After an hour or so, the nest building activity was over for the morning. The female disappeared and the male perched on a nearby branch, where it still was thirty minutes later. So I walked for a few minutes to our other favorite tree-dweller, a male Barred Owl. This beautiful owl was visible day after day in trees in the area where he could watch the cavity of a dead tree where his mate was sitting on eggs. This pair had used this tree in other years. They usually had from two to four owlets every year. When I discovered them, I was in time to watch the owlets once they had fledged. But this year I was looking forward to watching these owls daily once the owlets hatched. The male perched on trees near the nest every day was laid back and usually in sleep mode. It would open its eyes now and then and preen, but otherwise didn't move too much. On a couple of occasions it flew to another tree, and once it flew to the ground after a mouse or vole, which it didn't manage to catch. Most of its hunting occurred at night. These owls are nocturnal, as most owls are. Nevertheless, watching it take off to the ground, try to catch prey, and then return to the tree was wondrous. A glimpse into owl behavior, up close and personal. After watching the frenetic flying of the Cooper's Hawks, which streaked by above like bullets, the slow manner of the Barred Owl was in sharp contrast.

Once, as I watched the sleeping owl, one of the Coops suddenly swooped down from above, screeching, and buzzed the owl, which had awaken when it heard the Coop coming. The Coop almost bumped the owl and then landed on a nearby tree as the owl flapped its wings for balance. The owl didn't like this harassment. The Coop took off and flew at the owl again, which caused the owl to fly to another tree. The Coop made one more pass at the owl but the owl stood firm and didn't fly. The seemingly lazy Barred Owls are really very tough and superb hunters. The Coop would be in trouble if the owl caught it and the Coop knew that, which is why it flew past quickly and buzzed the owl, never getting close enough to be grabbed by the owl. Its speed was its safety. The Coop soon tired of this activity and flew away. The owl returned to sleep mode. The Coop intrusion was an annoyance, not a threat. My friend who watches the owls and Coops for hours every day told me that the harassment by the Coop was a daily occurrence. Some recreation for the hawk!

On another day, after watching the Barred Owl in sleep mode for a half hour, waking to preen a couple of times, I went back to the area of the new Coop's nest to hopefully catch them in action. As I approached the area of the new nest, I saw a raptor riding the thermals in circles above. It wasn't one of the Coops. It was a Red-tailed Hawk. Suddenly, from two different directions, the Coop pair flew out of trees like Tomahawk missiles and began to chase the Red-tail, screeching as they approached the hawk. The two Coops and the Red-tail were almost out of my sight when one of the Coops bumped the Red-tail. The Red-tail got the message and winged out of the area. A short time later, the Coops returned to the new nest area and perched on trees. They must have been tired after the morning of nest building and chasing the Red-tailed intruder away. I was proud of my Coops. They fiercely defended their territory and worked hard to build their second nest. Their work ethic was admirable. They were making that part of the forest ready and safe for the family they would soon bring into the world.

My lesson from these forest drama interludes is the power of nature. When in this environment I am totally immersed. The natural world and the wildlife it contains galvanize our attention and concentration when we are within it. There is no such thing as COVID-19 when one is witnessing a Bald Eagle taking off from a tree. Or a Cooper's Hawk pair building a nest. Or a Barred Owl swooping down to the ground after prey. It's why birding is the fastest growing activity in the country. People are addressing their need to escape the tribulations of our world. The universe of nature is where we can do this. Attain binoculars, an essential tool of this pursuit, and maybe a camera if photography is something of interest, and get out there. Leave COVID-19 and other troubling realities behind. Let the magic of birds lift you into their world.

John Harrison has been a book distributor for 45 years and is co-editor, with Kim Nagy, of Dead in Good Company--A Celebration of Mount Auburn Cemetery; *and three children's books in their* True Wildlife Adventure series: Skylar's Great Adventure, Star Guy's Great Adventure, *and* Big Caesar's New Home.

I Was Almost a Coronavirus Super Spreader
by Jesse Hercules

It started with the chills.

Friday March 6, 2020: I was out of town with my wife and our daughters, ages three and four. We were on an abbreviated Spring Break, a three-day weekend in St. Louis to visit my brother and his family. Sarah and Amelia had runny noses and cough, like all the other kids in preschool.

We'd spent all day at the new St. Louis Aquarium and the Magic House, a children's museum in Kirkwood. The kids were probably spreading snot and germs around, despite my best efforts to help them blow their noses and wash their hands. I knew that the Coronavirus was a serious concern in China, but it seemed many weeks away from being a problem here.

After dinner, we were back in our hotel room. Jennifer had some aches and soreness, which is not surprising for a mom who's been chasing two active little girls all over town. But then she put on a sweater. And got under the covers. "I'm really cold, all of a sudden." she said.

My thermometer was on the kitchen counter at home, three hundred miles away. Her forehead didn't feel warm, so I decided it wasn't a fever. Nothing else to do but get some sleep.

"I think I have the Flu."

Saturday March 7th: I woke up first, and thought I could get dressed and down to breakfast without waking the kids. Ha! Children will *never* let you do that. Pretty soon I was sitting in the hotel breakfast room with two kids, three plates, and a coffee.

The plan for the morning was to take Sarah and Amelia to their cousin's fifth birthday party. It was a special treat—they only get to see their three cousins a few times a year. They'd been looking forward to it all week.

Back in the hotel room, Jennifer was not feeling well at all. She was pale. Tired. She felt warmer. We decided I would take the girls to the birthday party and let Jennifer rest.

At my brother's house, the kids jumped into playtime with their cousins. Toys, watercolors, kick-scooters, and bikes with training wheels.

They all looked fine. Well, my kids and their cousins all had snotty noses. You wouldn't notice the coughs, with all the squealing and playing.

I got a call from Jennifer. "I think I have the flu." she said.

Urgent Care

"OK. I want you to get TamiFlu today if it's the flu. It can't wait until Monday," I said. I had a flashback to last fall, when I had to take Jennifer to the emergency room at seven p.m. on a Friday. Having two small kids whining and crawling on you while trying to get medical care for your wife is harder than it looks.

I asked my brother and sister-in-law if I could leave the kids with them. "Yes, you can absolutely do that," said my sister-in-law.

I drove back to the hotel and got Jennifer. We drove to the Urgent Care. She walked in, got a mask, and sat down. I collected the paperwork and started filling it out. She had a cough, congestion, fever, upset stomach. The doctor checked her lungs and examined her throat. He ordered a flu test.

"I think flu," he said. "The test came back negative, but probably if we gave it to you tomorrow it would come back positive." He wrote a prescription for TamiFlu and sent it to a local Target pharmacy. We got the medicine and some cups of Jell-O. I dropped Jennifer off at the hotel and went back to my brother's house to pick up Sarah and Amelia.

Off to the Zoo!

Jennifer was feeling worse. "I felt like I was going to die," she said later, looking back on that morning in the hotel room. She didn't think she could stand the long trip back to Memphis. I was not going to keep the kids in the hotel room, catching flu and climbing the walls all afternoon.

So I took them to the St. Louis Zoo.

"What do you want to see?" I asked. "Polar Bears!" said Amelia. There's no enthusiasm like a three-year-old's enthusiasm.

"I want to ride the train." said Sarah, with a shy smile. Got it. This was the child who was afraid of the tunnels last year. She's opening up.

How many hundreds of handrails, doors, and other surfaces did they touch and breathe on? Hard to say. At least as many as they did on the day before at the Aquarium and the hands-on activities at the Magic House.

90

Jennifer felt somewhat better by nightfall. The fever was under control with Tylenol, and we figured the TamiFlu was starting to work to combat the virus. We spent most of Sunday traveling back to Memphis.

It's Not The Flu

Amelia was a miserable three-year old by Sunday night. She had a fever to go with the runny nose and cough. She didn't feel like eating. I put her to bed with some ibuprofen to handle the fever while she slept.

By eight a.m. Monday I was at the pediatrician's office with Amelia. I explained that her mother had been diagnosed with flu and Amelia had the same symptoms. The doctor spent a couple of minutes telling me about how their new flu test was the earliest-detecting test on the market. "If it's flu, we'll know it," he said.

He asked some Coronavirus questions. "Any foreign travel? Any contact with people who traveled abroad?" No, and no.

The flu test came back negative. "So it's not flu, which is good news," said the doc. He advised me to just take her home and treat the symptoms with over-the-counter meds.

It Gets Worse All Week

By Tuesday, Amelia had a 102.7 fever. Jennifer was still sick. Clearly, the TamiFlu was not working. On Wednesday, Sarah had the fever also. "If it's not the flu, what is it?" I said.

My brother called. "I think my kids have a fever," he said. "They are definitely not feeling good."

I was almost a Coronavirus Super Spreader

So let's recap. I took my two children to the Aquarium, the Magic House, the Zoo, and a birthday party with a bunch of other kids. They touched and breathed on all kinds of surfaces that hundreds or thousands of other people must have touched that weekend.

As far as I knew on Monday, it could be Covid-19. Fever and all the flu-like symptoms, but two tests confirm it's not the flu. Covid-19 is contagious even before the fever appears, so my kids could have been spreading it widely in the days before the fever arrived. With fever and flu-like symptoms, but a negative flu test, experts would say it's time to do a Covid-19 test. But no tests were available in Memphis.

I felt like I was about to come down with something: fatigue, a hint of pressure in the lymph nodes, a little congestion. But nothing like the rest of the family was going through.

"Let's all stay home for the week," I said. "We can't get a Covid-19 test, and there's nothing the doctors can do if we have it." I dug into my stash of electronics and found a pulse oximeter I once bought. I put in some fresh batteries and it fired right up.

"If anyone's OxSat drops below 90%, we'll head to the hospital," I said. Meanwhile, the grocery stores and pharmacies were selling out as panic gripped the country.

Fifth Disease

By Thursday, Amelia's cheeks were really red.

She had just recovered from impetigo a week ago. The red splotches on her cheeks last week had quickly faded in response to some topical antibiotics. So I assumed the red cheeks were just the skin infection coming back again. Like every three-year old, the mucus that comes out of her nose gets rubbed around her face more than it goes into a Kleenex.

Jennifer posted a picture to Facebook showing Amelia's face. "Should I be worried?" she asked.

My mother, who had run a preschool for two decades, knew exactly what it was. "That looks like the slapped-cheek disease."

"What??" I said.

It was. I was quickly able to research Fifth Disease, a common childhood illness caused by a parvovirus. It's highly contagious, spreading through saliva and mucus. It starts with cough, fever, flu-like symptoms. After a few days, a distinctive rash appears. The pictures online show children's faces so red they look like they've been slapped. Hence, the nickname for the disease.

I called my brother. His kids had the rash, too. Sarah and Amelia's rashes had spread down to their arms and legs also, totally characteristic of Fifth Disease. I breathed a sigh of relief.

Fifth Disease in children is not serious. It clears up on its own, and kids make a full recovery. Adults can get it also, although many are immune if they had it when they were younger. I never got the rash, so perhaps I had a mild case.

Jennifer was probably exposed to Fifth Disease through her work as a preschool teacher. Then our kids got it from her. For medical reasons I won't go into here, Jennifer was more likely to get a serious case of it than most adults, and less likely to get the rash.

And Now We Wait.
It's now ten days later. Jennifer slept on the couch several nights so her coughing wouldn't keep me awake. She continues to have a low-grade fever. Two nights ago, she had an upset stomach and didn't eat. Is she still wrestling with Fifth Disease, or do we have something new?

Last night after dinner, I had a lot of joint and muscle aches. Surprising, since I hadn't done any exercise or physical work that day. My stomach was irritated. I had some chills, but my temperature was okay. About eleven p.m. Jennifer came into the bedroom, and I asked her to feel my forehead.

"Yep," she said. "You have a fever." I got the thermometer. It was 102.3 degrees.

Am I finally getting the Fifth Disease that everyone else had? It's a long-incubation illness. Or is it something else? Am I at risk of spreading a new illness to Jennifer and the kids, or am I the last to get the germs they already have? Time will tell.

But this time, we're all staying home.

Epilogue
March 24: Everyone's fever has subsided. Even the coughs are gone. We never had the opportunity to get tested for COVID-19. Even today, our local hospital only tests those meeting the CDC criteria (substantially sicker than we were). I'm betting Fifth Disease explains everything in our case. There are a lot of viruses that cause fever, cough, and a runny nose. We got one of them. And like most people, we got better.

Jesse Hercules is an engineer and technology entrepreneur living in Memphis, Tennessee.

View from Australia, "The Lucky Country"
by Rosalind Horton (Australia)

It's just three months since the terrible fires in parts of Australia, when for so many who lost everything it must have felt the end of the world. And now the unbelievable COVID-19 nightmare. We have never known anything like this. Across the Tasman, Jacinda Ardern, New Zealand's prime minister, took an earlier and much more restrictive stand than Australia. New Zealand is never afraid to stick its head up and I think is ahead of the game. New Zealand is in complete lockdown with people not allowed any contact out of their family or household "bubble," with most shops and businesses closed. The most distressing thing for me is that while the lockdown is in place I'm not able to visit my darling mother in Auckland in this latter part of her life.

Here in Sydney, New South Wales, Peter and I bunkered down at home, earlier than the rules suggested, but anyway it seems a no-brainer that the fewer interactions there are in the community, the faster that curve will flatten. Australia is supposed to be "The Lucky Country," but it will take more than luck to get to the other side of this.

In early March we packed up our Tvan that looks like a moon-pod, and headed south. We'd arranged to meet up with friends, Joe and Sandra, in Mallacoota, just over the NSW-Victoria border, for a week of music and a catch-up. They're a delightful couple whom we met in 2017 at Mission Beach, Far North Queensland. There, in freer times, we camped right by the beach as we summoned the courage to tackle the 4WD trip of 2300km return, into the orange dust up the rough roads of the magnificent Cape York Peninsula, right to Australia's tip. This courage-summoning required daily cracking of fresh coconuts, green paw-paw salad, music-making, chardonnay-drinking, and socialising with Sandra and guitarist/singer Joe. With Peter playing bass and me on fiddle and singing, and calling ourselves "Ros & the G-Strings," we played for fun at local bowling clubs. True highlights were watching the bowlers as they avoided the mass of ugly cane toads which swarmed and plopped across the bowling green, and the amazing suppers produced by the ladies who brought trayfuls of their best, old-fashioned baking.

Along the way to Mallacoota, we had beautiful stops at refreshing lakes and gorgeous, long, white uninterrupted beaches. It was shocking, though, to see the fire's devastation as we travelled south through NSW; homes and lives, shops and businesses in ruins amongst piles of iron and rubble around lone chimneys and burnt-out cars. So much of the bush was blackened and lifeless with countless exploded trunks, deafening silence, and no birds or animals. The bush and beach camping parks were missing the normal glorious racket of screeching, swooping cockatoos, wonderful parrots, rosellas, cheeky magpies. Hungry possums and koalas with patches of burnt fur searched for food at the wrong times and places. And yet, miraculously, in trees with entirely burnt, black trunks, new life was springing from the char, with the beginnings of ferns and undergrowth below. Ants' nests and insects were all getting going again in their tiny part of the world, which, after disaster, still recovers and regenerates.

Knowing that in the 1918 Spanish flu epidemic the NSW-VIC and NSW-QLD borders were closed, we decided to head for northern NSW, taking our ensuite toilet and shower so that we could set up completely off the grid. However, within a week all the camping parks were closed, along with most Australian borders. The result of this, by the way, is that there are now lots of "grey nomads" either who live on the road and have nowhere to go or are stuck in states not their own. Farmers and owners of large properties are generously offering places for people to camp, and maybe to help out on their farms.

We are mindful of the terrible potential consequences of the coronavirus for Australia's first people, the indigenous communities where remoteness makes preserving health in the face of this pandemic a massive challenge. The communities wisely took steps themselves, early, to seal their lives off from outsiders. The indigenous Elders are their guidance, wisdom, and traditional ancient knowledge, so the communities are protecting them, treating them like gold.

We'd planned a Tvan trip to Northern Territory and Arnhem Land. We were looking forward to that fun moment when, after a lot of hassle, we are finally packed up and can drive off into the unknown, towing our Tvan like a snail on our backs, signalling the start of the new trip by pressing the Go button on the CD player to hear two songs...Willie Nelson followed by Canned Heat singing "On the road again." That's how we've done it before, anyway. So simple, so much taken for granted, the huge and carefree drive through the outback of this magnificent land, stopping wherever we liked, now just a dream as we wait for the world to open up again.

In the meantime we're staying home. When I'm worrying about coronavirus I listen to podcasts, including a great gardening show about growing massively nutritious microgreens from broccoli sprouting seeds. So of course we're now growing microgreens...1g=500 seeds=10c a punnet. As well, we're creating a podcast-inspired straw bale vegetable garden. For once we'll be here for a whole veggie-growing season. We'll soon be coming in from the garden with great armfuls of fresh greens, glowing translucent complexions, long shining hair, throwing back our heads laughing with film star white-teeth smiles, beautifully manicured nails, slim waists, and muscly biceps. All the things you see in vegetable ads. It will be quite a transformation. In the meantime we are stuck with how we look, which is none of the above.

Normally our week is busy seeing family and friends, which always involves endless supermarket trips, dinners, barbeques, expanding the dessert repertoire, food experiments and recipe adaptations, admonitions from Peter about not trying new things on guests. However, all these delightful social interactions are on hold and in the quiet we're noticing that we're actually enjoying the lull.

A good friend once called our pantry an "archaeological dig," the layers representing our many interesting cooking crazes and mad phases over many years. We could start by sorting that out. There's so much to do. I'm practising piano. It's a great opportunity to get stuck into some violin practice, play some solo Bach, some bluegrass or gypsy jazz, or practise my little Merlin dulcimer thing, and learn a blues or two. Then there's my mandolin and slide guitar practice. Also, I have the kids' old high school maths textbooks out, via which I'm going to chisel my maths skills. There is my embarrassing one-cubic-metre collection of various lengths of exciting dress fabric to make up into fabulous garments. No shortage of projects, all requiring vision and discipline. The only snag is that we've instead got sucked in to watching the entire Breaking Bad over again.

This brings me to TV-watching, which I have never been any good at because you're supposed to keep still. We tried a Netflix subscription for a while. Do you know about the psychological state called Showverload? That's when all your available TV-watching time is used up channel-flicking and trying different silly films until exasperation and overwhelm set in, at which point, overloaded by the sheer weight of having to make a choice about which show to watch, you just give up and read a book. Showverload. Regarding risk minimisation around movies, have you considered that it's possibly better to just stick to the same, single show that you know is good, and watch only that? That way, there is no risk: You can't be disappointed and you haven't wasted any time. Win-win.

Our little granddaughter is a huge delight, bringing such joy and wonder as she grows. Our visits to her are replaced now with regular chats and FaceTime calls, Toytime with Peter and me doing silly acts and ridiculous voices without embarrassment, and reading stories. Very sad and strange not to be picking her up and cuddling her, but grateful for devices with cameras.

We reflect on the good, feeling grateful for the love and support of our families, siblings and partners, and good friends. We pare ourselves back, enjoy the simplest things and remind ourselves of how little we need. Meanwhile, Peter and I relish this very close time together.

Our children and now our little granddaughter are our greatest blessing. Our hearts are filled with love for them, and we are mindful and thankful every day for the joy and contentment that family brings to our lives.

Rosalind Horton is a former violinist with the Sydney Symphony Orchestra and passionate lover of garlic.

The Bird Cleaner: A Snapshot of the Future
by Stephen Hughes

Except for Sundays, Jason Hawkins drove his diesel Dodge Ram emblazoned with his company logo, ABC DISPOSAL, scouring every neighborhood in the Salt Lake Valley. ABC, at the top of the alphabet, stood for Acme Bird Cleaner, or as Hawkins liked to joke, Assorted Bird Corpses, and Hawkins was hustling to snatch up as many dead birds as possible. Each bird brought him $9.00 if it was clean. If it was diseased, the bird fetched $15.00. His list of clients was growing and his new wife loved it that his perseverance was bringing welcome financial relief, paying down their debts.

The first stop was Piccadilly and Curl's, a quaint, old-fashioned barbershop that did its best to keep its parking lot clean after recent upgrades to laser, wind, and solar tech. The adverse effects of these newfangled technologies resulted in more and more birds killed weekly. The numbers continued to climb, especially after local zoologists bred and released more birds to counteract their otherwise declining numbers. Yet, the recent Bird Flu in the east worried many. Quarantine suspicions grew, as did Jason's wallet.

His watch rang. His wife's concerned face was there and she said, "Jason, Aunt Jill called."

Aunt Jill was the receptionist at a chiropractic office. His wife didn't like to talk about work, so clearly the call was important.

"They need a bird cleaner. Today," she said. "Aren't you heading to Millcreek this afternoon?"

"Yeah. Okay. I'll fit them in. You told them our prices?"

"Yep. Sixty dollars a week, and that you dispose of the birds free!"

"I hope my clients never find out I sell the dead birds to Designer Corp to reuse. I've started to see some reanimated birds."

"How can you tell? Don't they all look the same?"

"They have a different shine to them. Almost like an oily sheen. Greasy in certain angles of light. They also feel different. Like paper that's been recycled too much. They feel rich."

"I think the word is oleaginous."

"My thesaurus wife with the English degree! Is that big belly going to get the smarts from you, too?"

Jason Hawkins, Bird Cleaner, got out of the truck at Piccadilly and Curl's and grabbed a shovel and five-gallon paint bucket. Anticipating the imminent arrival of their first child, he worked quickly. Every dollar of extra income would not only offset their debts, but would also help pay for the baby's delivery.

"Honey, I've got to get to work. Love you!"

"Love you, too!"

Jason scooped up eleven birds at Piccadilly's and Curls. One reanimated, two diseased, the rest clean. The usual gulls, jays, magpies. There was even one hummingbird. He was still awaiting a deal on reanimated birds, which were of an indiscriminately mixed species.

Driving from appointment to appointment could get boring. Yes, there was a constant playlist of music to listen to, but when even that got old, he had switched to podcasts. Though the flood of entertainment had its ups and downs, his inspiration for the business had grown out of that sea of free information. His self-appropriated learning and his burgeoning experience helped him grow his YouTube and Instagram pages as the leading voice in the Bird Cleaning Industry—an industry that a couple of years ago no one had thought of.

Hawkins, wearing his hazardous material suit, arrived at Aunt Jill's chiropractic office in the afternoon. It was clearly in desperate need of a bird cleaner. Dozens lay in the parking lot underneath wind turbines, several on grass with cut-off parts from the laser mowing service, and several fried from the solar tech attached to the roof and sides of their building.

The chiropractor, dressed in an untucked Hawaiian shirt and short khakis, approached Hawkins as he attached his face mask. He didn't actually need it since he had the shovel and gloves and washed himself routinely. However, the COVID-19 pandemic a few years before taught him that the mere perception of cleanliness was a prudent business practice.

"You here for the birds?" asked the chiropractor.

"Yeah, I'm the bird cleaner."

"Good, I can't risk any of my patients getting sick from these things. And with the tax write-offs I might as well do all the environmental tech stuff. Who wouldn't? It's a good deal."

Hawkins nodded his head since the man couldn't see his cheek muscles hook his smile into a falsified grin of agreement behind his face mask. He got to work and shoveled up dead birds. It was almost the end of the day and he still had to drive to Designer Corp Labs in West Valley City to drop off his collection. Before arriving there, he stopped for a restroom and snack break at a local Maverik gas station, where he organized the birds between clean, diseased, and reanimated.

The laboratory's campus was surrounded with a ten-foot brick wall with razor wire and glass on top. The secrets the lab held rivaled Willy Wonka's or Apple's. Security scanned the tag stickered inside his front windshield. He headed for building #26A—Birds.

Hawkins parked outside the loading dock and the bay door lifted open. Per routine, the lab operator, Hedge, was there to greet him. Like Hawkins, Hedge was dressed in a hazmat suit and facemask.

"If it isn't Mr. Hawkins, our favorite bird cleaner! What do you have today?"

Hawkins, exiting his Dodge, responded, "thirty-five clean, thirteen diseased, and three reanimated."

"Not a bad haul, Hawkins." Hedge began to collect them in the lab's hermetically sealed plastic containers.

"Hey, Hedge, I need to talk about money. I'm hearing from zoologists I can get the same fee, plus a tax write-off, if I go to the government, since they release the bred birds into the valley. Also, we haven't agreed on rates for reanimated birds yet. I want $20.00 for reanimated."

Hedge tightened his shoulders. "You don't negotiate Designer Corp rates with me. I have no say. You know that."

"I beg to differ. People learn about the trade from me, so you know very well that if I ditched Designer Corp and I posted it on social media, you'd lose a good seventy percent of your bird business. Look Hedge, we aren't friends. This is purely business. I don't really care for Designer Corp, and I know all about the whole Designer Baby project. I have a kid on the way that we did the natural way. So I think it would be in your interest to pay me a little of your tainted money.

Hedge pulled out his phone and typed into an app.

"Okay, it's done. You've got a deal. Let's take those damn birds off your hands!" said Hedge, with the same smile Jason didn't have to expose behind his own face mask.

Stephen Hughes is a freelance percussionist in Utah who has written stories since he was four years old. https://theprose.com/StephenLHughes

Equinox
by Tana Hunter

It's the Equinox. The spring one. The refreshing time of year when we leave the cold dark winter behind and rush to the sweet musical life of spring. I went mushroom hunting yesterday.

Today I woke up dead. I know, that sounds crazy. And when I died, I felt the deaths of all the living things that died at the same moment: the tree shattered by lightning, the bug eaten by the bird, the deer hit by the car. It was a fleeting moment that came with the sudden realization that life is sleepwalking, and death is the ultimate reality. Initial shock gave way to reality, and the amazement became release. Energy dissipates, spreads, and shares.

Enough of that! Turns out, you can keep your energy if you try hard enough. Thus ghosts.

And cats. Their energy is really hard to dissipate. They see ghosts, hear ghosts, and feel ghosts. So here I am, a bit of doughy energy, and the cats prickle, because now I know their secrets. I try to make the curtains move, the cats laugh. The black one walks up to the window and the curtains move in anticipation. With dogs, it's all about knowing what is going to happen; with cats it's knowing how to make it *not* happen.

I try to move through the window and it cracks. *Hmmmm.* My energy ball is too dense to go through walls unless I want them to explode. How do I get out of the house? The chimney! Up I go, and once out, I feel the great relief of liberation. I want to know what the birds are doing. I spy a hawk above and try to gain altitude to be near, but the hawk whisks away.

I have a few things to learn. Moving without losing energy is impossible. I'll need new sources so I can stay together, so I float, and the sun comes out from behind the clouds. *Whew!* Energy! I am refreshed! It's not really flying, what I am capable of, but more like willing my energy to move. I feel a bump and then a squish. I've absorbed the energy of a dead bird! But that makes me less of myself, diluting me and spreading me around. And I have unfinished business.

The day before yesterday, I finally got fed up with my next-door neighbor from hell. He's a hunter, trapper, poacher, and taxidermist. My dog once got caught in a trap set by another careless idiot and thankfully I had learned how to get her out because I was afraid of my neighbor setting them in his yard. Traps are indiscriminate, cruel and barbaric. When my neighbor was out doing his nasty business, I put on my hooded overcoat and went over there at night and set his biggest, nastiest trap where he would step in it when he came home. I waited to hear him scream but accidental mushroom poisoning beat me to the punch.

So now I am floating around waiting for it to happen. *Oops,* another entity just got absorbed, a squirrel eaten by my neighboring great horned owl. My horrid neighbor eats squirrels that he traps in his back yard, so I'm surprised the owl found one.

I'm aware of a truck going into the yard next door. The door opens and as he steps out, his left foot goes crunch in the trap hidden in the pile of leaves I hid it under. I hear bones break. I hear screams. I feel great satisfaction. I suddenly feel another entity: The poor bobcat in his truck just gave up the ghost. As interesting as it is to encompass all these animals, it's so diluting to me that I'm afraid I'm becoming a bigger part of the ether, and my satisfaction of getting even is less and less important. As I move off, as I absorb more entities and more energy from the sun, I dissipate more and more. It is a free feeling that I will soon become one with all the energy in the universe.

...merrily, merrily, merrily, merrily, life is but a dream.

Tana Hunter is a mother, house sharer with dogs, cats, birds, insects and a very patient husband.

Fiddler on the Porch—March, 2022
by Julie R. Ingelfinger

Yesterday, one of those sparkling early spring days with cloudless skies, I took a walk in my neighborhood. The streets remain still, with as little traffic, I imagine, as there was in the 1920s, when the nearby Huron Avenue fire station would put moss on Garden Street so that the sound of the fire wagons would not bother the residents in the posh section of town. I actually walked in the middle of the street for a while, and no car came by. The trees show signs of budding out, and plenty of fat robins plucked worms from grass on Cambridge Common.

Younger folks walked along the streets and parks, and some biked or used scooters. A few jogged by. They were nearly silent, and still moved away from each other like black and white scotty-dog magnets that repel. Playgrounds remain closed, despite the over-ready slides and swings. Feral cats have used the sandboxes, though. In the distance, on Avon Hill, a bagpipe was playing (maybe a wedding again, most of the funerals were over). And, as I walked down Garden Street, I heard a fiddler playing *Greensleeves.* He was old and frail, sitting in a green Adirondack chair that hampered his bowing. But he smiled and nodded from his porch. I waved; I think we both sensed we were old but had survived—some sort of miracle. I stopped and thanked him, and asked him his name. John, he said.

Some months back, when I could still fill my one prescription for enalapril and get over-the-counter stuff such as calcium and vitamin D—and batteries for my hearing aids, I felt that for someone "my age," I could still work remotely and come out the other side. We all thought so. And, like everyone, I wondered why the pandemic was happening and why now. Was it climate change that facilitated the transfer of COVID-19 from bats to humans? Was it, as some claimed, a lethal virus purposely let out of a nefarious laboratory? Or just fate? At first, I figured it would end soon; we'd bounce back to normal.

In the months before, in what little spare time I had, I was reading about the Mesozoic pedigree of birds, the mass extinction of dinosaurs and pondering the end of mammals, particularly, of course, humans. Would human extinction be anthropogenic? Or due to massive volcanic activity or, as many think with dinosaurs—a meteoric end? On the other side of the argument were "we" still evolving? But I believed curtains for humanity would be a long way off, centuries or even millennia after my great-great-great...great[nth] grandchildren had sauntered on and off the brief amphitheater of life.

My wondering about "big questions," which I ascribed to being at the north end of my 70s, turned out to be just months before the gurgling death of so many from coronavirus, the collapse of every corner of our human infrastructure, followed by the chaos. At the start, when electricity was still being "delivered" by EverSource, gas as well, we got news all day online, still ordered things, surfed the web and discounted reports suggesting that what is now reality might happen but probably would not. Good thing I downloaded the instructions for small solar generators for remote villages in Africa. Mine is working pretty well. It means I have a little light at night, which lets me read and helps keep away the urban coyotes, and maybe other beasts. And I also learned how to make a generator that hand cranks, so I can get online once a day and find out scraps of information when an occasional web browser and my server are both working.

I don't know if I have anything left in my bank accounts, as nobody is there to check for me. I ordered raised garden beds early, as the pandemic unfolded, so I do have some potatoes and a few other staples that may last through next winter. And I have some wood stashed in the cellar, if nobody takes it. Plus I have some canned goods left, and some outdated flour. I am not unique in this circumstance.

Meanwhile, I keep hoping that work may resume, for me and for others. Now? I still practice the piano, exhilarating at first, given so much free time without any commute, and still some solace; I work on learning to play the banjo I made two years ago. When the mood strikes me, I write down random thoughts like these.

I don't have any idea how many people are really left in Cambridge anymore. When I go on walks, most of the buildings look fine, except for the sections of town that had fires that the fire department couldn't reach, since gas for the fire engines was rationed and emergency calls rarely worked. There are tent cities there, and it looks like nobody has a good plan for what will happen when winter descends on us this year.

People have mostly stayed polite around here, which is a big surprise, at least to me. I would have thought there would be more desperate behavior and crime, though I suppose that, too may be coming.

The pandemic seems to have receded. By now nearly the entire population has had the virus, and, as with most viruses, people become immune. Further, when the next new virus jumps from animals to humans, it won't spread as quickly, since rapid global transportation has vanished.

We do get mail—the old way. And maybe it will be via horse and wagon, once cars are gone. My family survived, that is my children and grandchildren. But they live too far away for me to visit now. If train tracks get repaired, maybe I will be able to get to see some of them next year. Amtrak sent out an "official" note that there will be trains again, once the lines are physically fixed, now that the pandemic has receded. Hope so. I am almost eighty now.

This morning it looks as if it will be another nice day. When I've gotten going, I think I will take my keyboard, if I can get it to run on a cranked-up battery and put it in my shopping cart and go jam with the fiddler on the porch. John, he said his name was...

Julie Ingelfinger, a professor of pediatrics at Harvard Medical School (pediatric nephrologist) and a deputy editor at the New England Journal of Medicine by day (and sometimes night), gets a kick out of writing stories, poems and essays (and concert reviews), as well as playing the piano and learning to make stringed instruments in her spare time.

Capriccio Corona Da Capo
by Julie Ingelfinger

My second son got married last week, twenty-five years after the "Great Disruption" that changed life globally. How we make friends, see ourselves, have relationships, raise children, think about the past, the future and the moment were altered in a matter of weeks. But my son's wedding was traditional—attended by happy family and friends, and full of promise. It got me thinking about how little we understand, except when using a "retrospectoscope."

Upheaval—the disaster of COVID-19, the government planning now widely recognized as having been disorganized and too slow to respond, the exponential expansion of cases, horrific shortages, and enough fatalities within two months that pretty much everyone had someone important to them who was very ill or already gone—was pervasive. And yet, unexpected incandescent happiness still occurred, seemingly at random.

My uneasy awareness of the pandemic that erupted in Wuhan, China, began with lame jokes appearing in my inbox from "left coast" friends. In early 2020 there were just a few US cases—and still most, in Washington State, the first in a thirty-five-year-old man who had traveled to Wuhan and returned January 15th to become ill on arrival. There were others, some from a nursing home. There were none from Boston, not yet. So, I'd see a mask on a bottle of Corona, late night TV hosts doing monologues and figure, "this won't get like Wuhan." But soon COVID-19 was here—as we all know, and worse than in Wuhan, worse than in Italy. Before long, the populace was somber—involved or not. I was scared silly, not surprising, since my work as an Emergency Medicine physician meant I would be front and center when the pandemic reached us, expanded and peaked. I could see that here in the US "flattening the curve" so that cases would be spread out over time was no longer an option. And it wasn't.

I anticipated that weathering the logistics of the pandemic wouldn't be easy, since my ex, Paul, was also a doc—an infectious diseases expert who would be seeing some of the sickest patients. The two of us talked about what we'd do, hoping we would both stay well, given our boys, aged eight and six, who alternated weeks with us. "At least kids get mild cases," I thought. Well, most do, never mind why. And we were under forty, healthy, so not "high risk."

Paul and I talked with increasing frequency, given the kids, and the fact that our parents lived in other states, as did our siblings. It would be us and our nanny—if she did not get told to return home to Sweden, despite no lockdown there at first.

A good thing was that the past year had been less fraught with anger and obstinacy with my ex. I should be clear—we were both angry and obstinate, hard to know which of us more so. But we now collaborated, if uneasily, on how to raise the boys, and we were moving on with our lives. Or, it seemed we were. The kids were settled in to a routine, happy at school, and exploring various activities. Our nanny went with them to whichever of our homes they were on a given week.

We decided, Paul and I, to try to agree on what to do about the moving on in our lives bit. We were each seeing someone new--but not living with those somewhat significant others. I felt we should agree on a principle, but not demand change. Paul did not even want to talk about it. Of course, once school switched to online classes and home schooling, exploring life with a new partner presented various droll and awkward opportunities, and far fewer of them.

My boyfriend, Jim, was from Rowley, divorced but without kids, worked as a teacher at Phillips Academy in Andover and hated the drive to Boston. We both played the piano, liked to read, and to kayak and hike. At least his drives in to see me were against the traffic. But it was getting to be a strain. Jim didn't really understand what being a doctor entailed, and he was horrified that I would soon actually see patients with COVID-19. Jim and I decided to declare a moratorium on our relationship, even after all the students were sent away from Andover for the rest of the year. Maybe our friendship would have slowed down and ended anyway. But it seemed increasingly remote—and, frankly, meaningless.

Paul had a girlfriend. I knew nothing about her, except that she had no children, though she'd once been married. I never asked about her—I didn't think I cared. Paul seemed happier since he'd met her. Her name was Samantha, and the boys, who had met her a few times, called her Sam. She was very outgoing. Perhaps too outgoing for social distancing. I worried that Sam might get coronavirus, give it to Paul and the kids. Apparently, Paul worried as well. When they broke up, he seemed sad, but not for long.

Without adequate testing for the first weeks, we had no idea who had "it," and every slight twinge, sneeze or ache might signal "the start." Even working at Mass General Hospital we could not all get tested. By the end of March, a survey by Suffolk University and the Boston Globe showed that Massachusetts citizens were united in their commitment to adhere to strict and difficult isolation measures that then Governor Charlie Baker imposed on the state. And arrivals in the state were to quarantine themselves for fourteen days. All of them. Flights out of the US were now hard to find. Our nanny's parents back home in Sweden urged her to return home, and we helped her find a flight, one of the last to go.

So, there we were, without childcare and having many tiring shifts at our hospitals. With maneuvering we were able to coordinate our in-hospital work to be on alternating days, which meant one of us could be home at all times. On the rare days that both of us were home, we would go on an outing with the kids, to a trail, or to a beach, while the beaches were still open. And we practiced what was labeled as "social distancing." To my amazement, we agreed on a curriculum for home schooling, and we found ourselves agreeing on more and more things, beyond the kids.

The pandemic kept getting worse for over a year, at which point a vaccine was approved and put the brakes on the vast epidemic. By some miracle, neither Paul nor I contracted COVID-19. But half of our clinician friends did. Some were gravely ill. A few died. I still cry when I remember intubating my best friend, who did not survive. Most of us were emotionally numb for years, at least in that realm.

As I said, life has never been the same. For us, it got better—and worse, depending. Much to our surprise, Paul and I rediscovered why we had once loved each other. And to our greater shock, that we still did. We have now been back together for twenty-five years, though we declined to get married again.

We know we are among the lucky ones.

Julie Ingelfinger, a professor of pediatrics at Harvard Medical School (pediatric nephrologist) and a deputy editor at the New England Journal of Medicine by day (and sometimes night), gets a kick out of writing stories, poems and essays (and concert reviews), as well as playing the piano and learning to make stringed instruments in her spare time.

And Now, a Word
A Fable for Children of All Ages
by Janet K. Linder

"Why do we have to keep washing our hands?!"

The fourth graders at Corona Avenue Elementary School were lining up on the black top, waiting to wash their hands at the outdoor spigot before going back to their classrooms. They had just finished their daily kickball game on the field. The kickball game itself was pretty pathetic—everyone had to stay six feet away from everyone else, no throwing the ball, only kicking it if it came near you in the field, and no tagging anyone out.

David didn't like being called a complainer, but between the hand-washing every twenty minutes, the so-called kickball game that was really just an excuse for running around, and no one really explaining what was going on, he couldn't help opening his mouth.

"Mrs. Simms, how come our desks are so far apart? Why do we have to eat lunch spread out in the hallway? When can we go home?"

The last question was the scariest. Ever since Monday afternoon, when Principal Williams announced that kids had to stay in school overnight, sleeping in the gym in sleeping bags that mysteriously appeared, they had all been stuck at Corona Avenue School. Cafeteria fish sticks and mealy apples were getting old. The school ran out of ice cream after three days.

Outside, things looked normal, but the streets were pretty quiet, with few cars on the road. Parents called kids on their phones to say everything would be alright, they'd see them soon. But by Thursday, everyone was getting antsy. The students had watched movies about space, sea turtles, and "How our Government Works," had dance parties (six feet apart), and tried to sit still during quiet reading time, which mostly consisted of kids trying to make each other laugh from a distance. Math had gone out the window entirely.

By Friday, David wanted answers, and wanted his friends to help him get them.

"Alex, we've got to get to the bottom of this," David said as they walked back into the building. "Let's try to sneak into Principal Williams' office and see what we can find out."

"Are you crazy?" said Alex. "If they find us, we'll get sent out to the hallway to sit alone, and have to wash our hands twice as often."

"Just come with me, come on," David answered. He started to lag behind his class at the end of the line.

"Okay, but this better be fast!" Alex also hung back.

When the class turned the corner and started down the long hallway, David and Alex hugged the wall and started slowly creeping toward the principal's office next to the nurse's room and the main entrance. They were almost at the office when the main door opened and Lisa, the fifth grade class president, walked in. She was allowed out to check the weather twice a day and make sure no kids had escaped.

"Look serious!" David whispered to Alex.

"Oh, hi Lisa, we're just going to the nurse to get more hand sanitizer."

"Hmmm," said Lisa. "I thought each class had twenty-five bottles. You can't be out this soon. What are you two up to?"

"I'm serious, Lisa. A kid barfed from eating too much tuna melt, and we had to use five bottles to clean up the mess."

"Well, you better get back to your rooms soon. And don't stand so close to each other!"

After Lisa disappeared down the hall, David and Alex peeked inside Principal Williams' door. No one was there. *Whew.* They must be in a meeting.

"All clear, now's our chance." signaled David.

They crept inside the office and started searching the principal's desk, his desk drawers, even the pockets of his suit jacket hanging over his chair. Nothing suspicious, no clues, no answers. David was about to give up, when he saw the email still up on the principal's screen. From the Governor! David and Alex peered closer to read the letter.

Dear Principal Williams,

Trust me, this weird virus is under control. Everything will be just fine very soon, maybe even better than things have ever been before. We'll all be back to normal, and all of you will be so grateful to me. I am sending this top-secret email only to certain places, to give you an important message: You work somewhere that has the name "corona" in the title, so you might still be in danger. This virus is nasty, a real snake. The word corona itself can spread the virus, or so some people have told me. So anyone inside a building or factory or beer company, for example, that has the word corona in it, must not come near any of the rest of us! Keep away from me, and my family, too!

From, the greatest Governor the world has ever known.

P.S. Remember, this email is top-secret and confidential. Do not forward or print.

David and Alex couldn't talk. Then they looked at each other and burst out laughing.

"I don't know who is dumber, Williams or the governor!" David said. "Even a lowly fourth-grader knows viruses are microbes that attack living species in order to replicate. They can't invade *words*!"

The boys ran screaming down the halls, "It's a hoax, it's a hoax! We can all go home!"

And everyone did. The next year, the name of the school was changed to the John Dever School, after a retired superintendent. Kickball came back, but the cafeteria still served too many soggy fish sticks.

Janet Linder graduated from Corona Avenue Elementary School in Valley Stream, New York, long before there was email.

Smoked
by Cheryl Marceau

"Whatcha doing?" Pete asks. "You been staring at that phone, not saying nothin'."

"Nothin' to say," Richie answers. He Googles intently, holding the phone off to one side so Pete can't see.

They're in Pete's dented rusty pickup, parked on a dirt logging road north of McAdam, New Brunswick, close to the Maine border. It's late afternoon, nearly time for the shift change at the US border crossing in Vanceboro, Maine.

Pete grabs for the phone, but Richie yanks it out of the way. "So why won't you show me?" Pete taunts. "You got a hot new girlfriend? You finally gettin' laid?"

Richie's face burns. He hopes it doesn't show. "Shut it, Pete. None of your damn business."

Pete smirks. "Well, get focused on our business or we are screwed. Now what's our story again? Say it like I'm the customs guy."

"We had a couple days off, came up here to see the train station. My old man always talked about it; he loved the trains." Richie has to give it to Pete. This is a good cover story about the huge train station in McAdam. Pretty famous in the old days, lots of train geeks come to see it. The beauty is, it's near the border, practically in the middle of nowhere. Less border patrol agents, less cops.

Richie still feels the heat in his face. His hands tremble. He knows Pete can tell, even though he tries hard not to let it show. "See, man? I'll be fine. Just worry about yourself."

Pete looks sidelong at him for a while, says nothing.

Richie closes the web page he's been looking at. Using his phone in Canada will cost him a fortune, but he needs to know what will happen if the customs officer finds the other stuff he's bringing across the border, that Pete doesn't know about. Anyway, his cut for doing this job will be way more than the stupid cell phone charge.

Pete puts the truck in gear and pulls forward.

"Where are we meeting these guys?"

Pete grins. "I got a great place worked out. Logging tract, hasn't been worked for a while so it's overgrown. Road's pretty hard to spot. Couple miles past the sign for Codyville Plantation. Found it hunting last fall. About as sweet as it gets. Cops'll never find us."

Richie's gut churns. He tries but fails to hold back the fart that erupts.

"Jeez! Richie!" Pete fans the air with his hand. "What the hell?"

"I can't help it, man. Must have been that sandwich." He pigged out on Montreal smoked meat when they stopped for lunch. "Hey, Pete. What if the border guards check our story and find out we haven't been to the train station?"

"They won't check our story because they'll believe us and we'll be down the road. Will you stop acting like an old lady?"

Richie gazes out the window at the unbroken line of pine trees in a stretch of woods not yet logged. Nothing to see but the dirt road ahead of them and the trees all around. No signs, no buildings, no people. Maybe it would be better if he headed off through the woods, except he can't or the buyers would hunt him down like an animal.

He thinks about his brother Connor, who put him onto this deal. Connor joined the Army out of high school. All Richie ever hears from their mother is how he should make something of himself, like Connor. But when Connor got out of the Army he just got some crappy job in Bangor. His buddy Pete got them into this little business on the side. Connor is supposed to be on this trip, but he had to work an extra shift at the last minute, so he talked Pete into taking Richie instead. After the way Connor saved his butt on their last run to Canada, Pete owes Connor a favor.

The truck bounces on the deeply rutted road. Richie needs to get out before he shits himself. "Hey Pete?" Pete stares ahead, wrestling the steering wheel to dodge potholes. "I gotta stop."

Pete's face darkens. "We don't have time."

Richie can't keep going. What if he has an accident in the truck? "I gotta stop, Pete. For real."

Pete slams on the brakes and Richie lurches forward before the seat belt pulls him back. "Get outta here," Pete says. "I'll wait five minutes."

Richie climbs out of the truck and runs into the trees so Pete won't see him. Nothing happens, but his gut is still going crazy. He checks his watch and goes back to the truck.

They return to the paved road and on toward McAdam.

Richie pulls out his phone again. "Pete?"

No answer.

"They got dogs at the border?"

"I don't know, maybe. What's it to you? We got everything wrapped up real good, dogs won't find it."

"What if they do? I can't remember if there were dogs at the other crossing in Houlton when we came north." If dogs sniff around, they'll find his personal cargo.

"Don't screw this up by thinking too much. I do the talking. You only open your mouth if they ask you a direct question."

Richie leans his head against the door, feeling the cool glass of the window on his cheek. He is nervous of the border crossing, but really scared of Pete and the buyers in Maine. Tears run down his face. He hopes Pete doesn't notice as he wipes them away.

"Are you crying?" Pete slams the brakes and shoves the truck into Park. "Listen to me right now. I am not saying this one more goddamn time. If you mess up this deal, I'll hurt you so bad you will beg me to kill you. I don't give a damn if you're Connor's brother. Clear?" Richie nods and wipes his face again. Pete gets the truck moving down the road, muttering. "We're already late. The guys'll think we bailed on them if we don't get there soon."

Richie can barely hear Pete for the hammering in his head. He sees a highway sign. McAdam, 4 km. They pass a few houses. Pretty soon they'll reach town, and then the border.

"Stop!" Richie sobs as he yells to Pete. "Stop the truck! I can't do it!"

"You stupid shit, what are you talking about? You are a dead man." Pete screeches to a stop at the side of the road. He jumps out, goes to the passenger side, grabs Richie's shirt and yanks him out of the truck, slams his fist into Richie's gut. "What is wrong with you?" Pete screams, spit flying from his mouth. He shoves Richie against the truck. "I shoulda never agreed to bring you in on this. What the hell was Connor thinking?"

Richie sniffles, snot running down his face. He's watching himself from somewhere else, knowing he's going to die out here.

"Answer me, you stupid shit!" Pete is hoarse. He yells so loud that someone must be able to hear him. But they're in the middle of nowhere. Nobody will hear.

"I got some of that meat in that town back there," Richie says.

"What's that got to do with anything?"

"When you went to that grocery store to get something for your headache? I got some of that Montreal smoked meat. Like they had at the diner. It was wicked good." He sniffles and wipes his nose with his sleeve. "I think it's illegal to take it across the border. Dogs will smell it for sure."

"You idiot! We gotta get rid of that damn meat."

"I'll throw it out, Pete."

"Yeah, buddy." Pete's voice is calm. Too calm.

As Richie takes the plastic grocery bag full of meat from behind his seat where he stashed it, he hears the driver's door open. He walks into the woods a ways off the road and tosses the bag as far as he can, then hurries back. Just now when Pete was yelling at him, Pete sounded scared. This worries Richie more than anything else so far.

Pete leans on the passenger door, smoking a cigarette. He throws the butt to the ground as Richie returns, and climbs in.

The truck approaches the border crossing.

"They got dogs!" Richie hisses. "Shit!" A border guard stands at the customs building, a police dog next to him.

Pete ignores Richie and pulls forward to where the guard waits. Richie tries hard to control his breathing. He spits on a paper napkin and swipes at the snot on his face.

Pete hands their passports to the guard without waiting to be asked, all casual like he crosses the border every day. Richie attempts to look just as casual.

"What was the purpose of your visit, sir?"

Pete answers just like they practiced. "We're big train fans, up to see the train station over in McAdam."

The border guard looks at them a long moment then back down at the passports. Richie wonders if they really look like the train geeks who come through. "How long were you in Canada?"

"A couple days."

"Where do you live?"

"Lincoln, Maine," Pete says. "Well, not really in Lincoln, just outside town. My buddy here lives in Chester."

The guard looks at Richie's passport. "Is that correct, sir?"

"Uh..."

"That's right," Pete answers for Richie.

"I asked your friend." The guard's tone is easygoing but he's standing a little straighter.

"Y-yes." It's all Richie can do to speak.

"Are you bringing back anything from Canada?"

Richie squirms. His stomach roils as he holds in the fart that he can feel coming. Just another minute and they're home free.

"Nothing," Pete answers.

The guard steps inside the building for a moment, gives the truck a once-over when he returns. He looks directly at Richie. "Is everything okay?"

"My friend here got greedy with the pies at the station," Pete says. "They got great pie. I think he's a little green around the gills, if you know what I mean." He laughs.

The guard ignores Pete. He frowns at Richie. "Sir?"

Richie freezes. A long, rumbling, stinky fart explodes from deep inside him. The dog strains at his leash, whining, lunging at the truck.

The border guard peers into the truck. "If you would, sir," he says to Pete, "please move your truck over there and step out."

"Absolutely, officer. Is there a problem?"

"Just pull over to that parking space and both of you please get out of the vehicle."

Richie is terrified of jail, but more terrified of Pete's connections and what they'll do if he and Pete don't show up. There's no way Pete can talk his way out of this. Richie squeezes his eyes tight and prays for a miracle.

The truck lurches forward. Richie can't bear to look.

"Stop!" the guard calls to them.

Richie sneaks a glance at Pete, whose eyes dart between the road ahead and the rearview mirror. They race as fast as the dilapidated truck can move, jolting over potholes and frost heaves, away from the border and into Maine.

Moments later a siren wails behind them. The border patrol. He and Pete are as good as busted. Pete swerves around an old sedan on a curve. The siren sounds farther away as they speed down the road.

"Look for a sign," Pete says. "It's orange, says keep out." Richie spots an orange blur just as Pete veers the car hard right onto a dirt road covered in undergrowth, the track barely visible. They drive deeper into the woods until Pete slams to a stop.

"Where are we?" Richie asks. Pete wordlessly pulls his rifle from its hiding place behind the seat and jumps out. Something rustles like a large animal in the trees. Two men in camouflage gear come out of the woods and walk toward him. The three of them huddle, glancing at Richie a few times. It doesn't feel right. One of the men brings him a large backpack. "Start packing it up."

Richie retrieves small wrapped parcels from their hiding places in the truck and stuffs them into the pack. When the first pack is full, the same guy hands Richie another pack, then another and another. Pete and the two camo guys hoist the packs onto their backs. The last pack sits on the ground next to Pete.

The siren has stopped. They've lost the border patrol.

"Pete here tells us you bought some smoked meat," the other camo guy says. It seems like he's in charge. "Shoulda brought some for us."

"That's a good one, smoked meat," the first guy says, laughing at his own feeble joke.

Richie's heart thuds. Nobody makes a move to give him that last backpack.

"Get in the truck," Pete orders.

Richie does as he's told. He smells raw gas and sees the guy in charge coming from behind the pickup with a gas can.

"Stay put!" Pete orders, as Richie tries to get out. Pete fishes a roll of duct tape from under the driver's seat, keeping his eyes on Richie. "Hands on the wheel!" He tapes Richie's wrists to the steering wheel as the guy with the gas sloshes it all over the pickup. Pete backs away as the other guy pulls out a lighter, flicks it, and tosses it in the truck.

Richie shrieks and pulls at the tape but he can't break free. Tears stream down his face. Burning to death is the worst thing there is. Damn Connor to hell for mixing him up in this.

"Drop the guns!" a new voice yells from the edge of the woods.

From out of nowhere, a guy in SWAT gear appears beside Richie and slashes the tape on his wrists. "Run!" he says, pulling Richie out of the front seat.

Richie stumbles from the truck and rolls away.

A blur of uniforms sprint toward Pete and the camo guys. Another uniform throws himself on top of Richie, seconds before the truck bursts into a fireball.

The SWAT officer on top of Richie pulls off his balaclava.

"W-what the hell?" Richie says as he realizes what he's seeing. "Connor? You're a goddamn narc? You freakin' set me up, man!" Richie takes a swing but misses, tries to shove Connor off him, swearing at him. "I was gonna die, you asshole!" He feels something stinging and gropes his face. His eyebrows are singed. He tries to wrestle away from Connor, who grabs him to keep him from tumbling into the bonfire that was Pete's truck.

"Sorry, buddy," Connor says, letting go of Richie. "We've been onto these guys for a while, just needed to catch them in action." He points to Pete and the camo guys, now handcuffed and closely guarded. "We bugged Pete's truck and tracked the GPS in your phone. I had a pretty good idea where the meet would be, but you really helped, getting Pete to make those stops. Gave us more time to get in place."

Richie is still furious, trying to land a punch. "I was this close to being burned to a crisp!"

"I'd never let anyone make smoked meat out of my brother," Connor says, snickering. "Okay if I call you Smokey?"

Cheryl Marceau, whose latest published story was "Payback With Interest," in Malice Domestic 13: Mystery Most Geographical, has traveled extensively in the US and Canada, but has never (knowingly) brought anything illegally across the border. https://www.sistersincrime.org/members/?id=28966610

Distance
by Julia Moser

The moment the train doors slid shut behind me, half the particles of air surrounding my face were replaced by something that smelled like chlorine. I curled my fingers up against the fabric inside the leather gloves that probably wouldn't protect me, taking quick, controlled steps to a spot one seat away from the end of the car and five away from the door. The plastic presses through the fabric of my jeans as I sit, little blue ridges, cold from disinfection.

The trains will probably close down tomorrow.

There are two other people in the compartment, both pointedly staring at the walls or their phones. No one is breathing much. No one wants to be on this train.

A phone starts vibrating, startling the air with angry pulses, and its owner grabs it out of a big black bag and swipes almost frantically to answer it. His voice is sharp in the heavy static silence of the train car, even as he softens and rounds his words for the high-pitched ghost of a voice on the other end. I feel the weight of my own phone in my pocket, and then the weight of the gloves on my hands. I'll call home as soon as I get to the station.

Nobody looks at the man on the phone. A poster on the wall across from me smiles and reminds me to wash my hands, but its edges are wrinkled and slightly yellowed as if people have been brushing against it for weeks, spreading their own little handfuls of disease.

My skin prickles.

At the other end of the compartment, the woman who had been sleeping with her head resting sideways on the window sits up straight in her seat. Her hand goes first to the collar of her coat, then to her backpack, then to the railing next to her, and her face stiffens. My eyes track every movement she makes, and I wince a little, sensing the stream of microbes that flows over her bare fingers when she touches the metal. The man across from me isn't on the phone anymore, and I try to go back to staring at walls, but the woman doesn't sit still, and I can't stop myself from noticing.

She half-leans forward, like she's going to stand up, but then changes her mind, craning her neck anxiously to look around the train car. Without exactly meaning to, I scan the car too, wondering what she sees that would be worth so thoroughly disturbing the stillness, but there's nothing except the two of us, the man with the black bag, and the chilly plastic walls. The woman stops looking and awkwardly shifts in her seat, tapping her feet around on the floor like she's feeling for something other than the blue tiles and thin layer of dust that collects in the corner behind her. I don't mean to keep watching her, but when she finally looks up, my eyes meet hers instantly. Her mouth starts to open, maybe to say something to me, but I blink and quickly turn my head to the other side.

For all she knows, I didn't even see her. I breathe in much more deeply than I have been, trying too hard to feel natural, and it almost makes a sound. My jaw snaps shut. The air is full of cleaning products and whatever was in the lungs of whoever breathed it before me, and thinking about it makes the inside of my skin feel like tiny grains of shifting sand.

The woman clears her throat, and everyone jumps a little. I try as hard as I can not to make eye contact again, but when she does it again I flinch visibly, and the third time I turn, almost expecting to see her doubling over, coughing blood into a tissue. Instead she looks impossibly uncomfortable with two pairs of eyes on her as she restlessly picks at her nails.

"I'm so sorry, but has anybody seen a pin?"

Her voice is crackling, almost a whisper. Maybe like she's about to cry.

The man across from me looks concerned. "A pin?"

"Sorry," she repeats, "a pin. An old one. It's gold, and it has a little horse on it." Her words lift so that every sentence sounds like a question.

I shake my head. The man does, too.

"No, I haven't. I'm sorry." He sounds sincere, which is more than I could do. After a moment, though, we've both turned away. There's a nervous knot in my stomach as I make a mental list of everything I've touched today. It shouldn't be too far to my stop.

A moment later, though, she's on the floor, putting her unprotected hands all over the dirty tile, and my gaze snaps back to her with a fascinated horror.

"What are you doing?!"

The man jumps to his feet, moving closer to her. "Are you sure you couldn't have left it back at the station?"

"No! I mean--" Her head snaps up. "The station will be closed after today... no, it's on here, I'm sure."

The man pauses, breathing deeply.

"Okay."

He gets down on his knees next to her and starts looking under seats where there is obviously nothing to look for, his hands darting in and out quickly, without touching anything. She stops for a second and watches him like she doesn't understand what's happening, and then turns hopefully towards me.

I wince and give her a shrug. "I really shouldn't. I'm going to stay with my aunt, and she's definitely old enough to be at risk. I'd hate to get her sick."

The woman's face relaxes, and she nods and says something about the grandmother who gave her the pin and how worried she is about her, but my stomach gets even tighter as I think about the empty one-person apartment I'm really on my way to. Why can't I just stop and help this woman look for some pin? I wouldn't even have to touch anything. Watching them on the floor, though, so close to so many germs that could get inside them so easily makes me want to drench the whole train in hand sanitizer before we're all full of swarming little viruses.

I swallow hard. The man is trying to make her laugh, and it's working a little bit. The blur of blacks, grays, and blues that streak past in the window glare back at me until I have to look away, at the floor, the silver railings, anything. Every inch of my body tingles with the possibility of contamination, infection.

When the man has to get off a few stops later, he shoots me a look over his shoulder that turns the air even stiller than it was when I first got onto the train. Inside my gloves, my hands are clenched so tightly I think I might scream, but I smile at the woman sitting on the floor.

"Do you think there's anything I can do?"

Her sigh is completely defeated, with traces of tears. "It's okay. If it was here we would've found it by now, and I only have one more stop anyway."

I purse my lips. "Maybe they'll find it tomorrow and call you if you let someone know?"

"Mmm."

They won't. There's no use. There will be big machines and chemicals and a smell of complete sterilization, and then the trains and the stations will sit, sealed off, for months before anyone can go back inside. If her pin is here when she leaves, she's never going to see it again.

I almost reach out to touch her shoulder.

"Did you say it was your grandma's?"

The woman nods, running a hand through a few short strands of hair. "I borrowed it when I went to stay in France about a year ago, and just never gave it back. I was supposed to be going to see her for a while now, but then she got sick—" Her voice catches, and my hands unclench. "Anyway, I'm going home, and I guess the pin isn't such a big deal. I just can't believe I lost it."

Trying to suppress the crawling in my skin, I lean closer to her, then realize I don't know what to say.

"I'm sorry."

She shakes her head. "It's not my fault."

That isn't the point, but I don't fight her. Instead, I fight my conflicting urges to hug her and move as far away from her as possible, settling on a safe, sad silence.

There are germs filling the air when she says, "I know you have to be really careful, but would you mind..."

"No, of course."

"Just quickly?"

I nod, and realize that I do want to help. "I know we'll find it."

And soon, I am walking on top of the rows of seats, peering into cracks and prying open gaps with my thickly gloved fingers while the woman follows along, fervently searching every inch of the floor. She doesn't grab my hand when I almost fall, but her flat palm stops an inch under mine, never coming any closer but following along, promising to catch me if I slip. Something golden glints in between two seats, and I grin.

"Hey!"

She jumps up, almost laughing, until I pull out a shiny fountain pen and my stomach falls.

"Oh. Sorry."

The woman nods and half-smiles at me, and then the intercom dings, signaling the doors to slide open and let her out. I wish her luck, and she tries to pretend not to quickly look around the compartment one last time before she's back on the platform and the train gives off a jolt, knocking me off my feet back into the filthy floor.

After a few minutes, I stand up and brush the dust off my jeans, then make my way back to my seat where I take off my gloves to apply too much hand sanitizer to every inch of exposed skin. I slip the pen into my pocket; maybe someone will need it, or maybe I'll run into whoever left it here in the first place.

A few times, I think I see a glint of gold in a crack under a seat.

Every time, I investigate, and every time it is my imagination.

The train rolls westward, smelling like chlorine, carrying me home.

Julia Moser is a junior at Eastchester High School. She's loved writing for as long as she can remember, and otherwise spends her time either in rehearsal for various musicals or hanging out with her pet rats and chinchilla.

Love in the Time of Corona
by Kim Nagy

Whoever envisioned a shopping quest for toilet paper? Or that toilet paper would become *the* destination item? That such trips morphed into expeditions because we often had to travel to more than one store to find some? Whoever thought toilet paper would become *rationed* and there would be a customer limit to purchases? If I bought some in the afternoon, could I buy it again in the morning? Was that hoarding?

As I turned into the Trader Joe's parking lot in Nashua, NH, wondering if I would be able to buy my usual twelve-pack or more likely nothing at all, I spotted an osprey flying low in the sky. As I drove closer to the store, I saw a second osprey sitting on a lamp post. Could it be?

Last year, a pair of ospreys had built a nest on a light post in the parking lot. They successfully raised two chicks. Photographing them had been fun, and the local paper published a few of my photos. The sense of community was strong, as people came from far away to witness this somewhat unusual event, and many people discussed the osprey's activities both in Trader Joe's and in other businesses located in the mall. Had they returned to build another nest and raise another family?

Ospreys, like many animals and birds, mate for life, but in the autumn, they migrate south separately. Upon return to the nesting grounds in the spring, the first arriving osprey waits for the other. There is always the threat of injury or death. They generally return to the same site, where they build a new nest.

Last year, my mother died unexpectedly. Her death had been tough, but there had been some emotional cushion. I had just returned from a Florida business trip with a personal day tacked on, where I photographed a family of otters; one of the best, unexpected wildlife photography encounters ever. So, I was really happy, until I wasn't. The memory of that trip softened the blow of her death, just a little bit.

A few days later, completely unexpectedly, I lost my executive job of seven-plus years after finishing my best quarter ever, after a multi-year track record of increased sales.

A very dark time followed, but there was another cushion. It was spring. I spent my jobless time well, and watched wildlife through the lens of a camera. I was searching for new ways of looking at old problems, and that made me focus on more positive outcomes. The weather was spectacular, and there was so much wildlife to photograph.

It was a difficult adjustment to go from a high-travel regional sales manager job to having nowhere to go. And today, one year later, I was in nearly the same situation, even though I had another job. Luckily, I had found a wonderful opportunity within a short period, and was now a national sales manager. I was looking forward to even more travel. But because of the coronavirus, most all business travel was grounded, as trade shows and events were cancelled; the future remained uncertain.

How strange to spend the first-year anniversary of my mother's death back in Nashua, not *just* to look for toilet paper, but certainly hoping for some. The coronavirus had made life very different. Words used to describe this event were: *unprecedented*, *once-in-a-lifetime*, *record-setting*; and not in a good way. The very best economy America had had in decades: with record low unemployment and a historically high stock market, had come to a sudden and violent cessation. In many ways, it seemed like the cure—sheltering in place and shutting down most businesses—was worse than the virus; it was like another death.

We learned new words: *social distancing*, *self-isolating*, *sheltering in place*. I first heard that last term when visiting a butterfly farm in Florida; in bad weather, they shelter in place, the brochure had said.

The media reacted as it often did; heavier on fear and emotions than facts. Like how they often hype up weather events ("Potentially the worst storm in history!") that turn out to be nothing. But this; *this*...the novel corona virus could kill...nearly everyone! The media seemed...gleeful in their breathless reports, which were non-stop negative. They frequently

129

showed a certain graph—a map of the world with pulsing red circles depicting virus cases—all over! Everywhere! No place was safe!

No one talked about how to strengthen the immune system.

Did anyone notice that the graph was a single vanity data point with no context; a map of the world, drenched in red circles? No numbers, no metrics, no matter. Networks kept showing it (" *We're all going to die!*"). No mention that 7,452 people died *every day* in the United States; one American every twelve minutes. Why wasn't that ever reported?

I feared the economic shutdown more than the virus itself. How long was this going to go on?

Back to looking for toilet paper in Trader Joe's. There was none. A cheerful team member told me that they usually sold out by three o'clock, but that day had been especially busy, and they had sold out early. Crestfallen, I went to the cashier with my other purchases. That cheerful clerk apparently found a six-pack, and he brought it over to me. It was as if he had gifted me with something wonderful and it made me feel very lucky indeed.

I mentioned the ospreys to the cashier. He didn't know they were back, but the news clearly made him happy. Even the employees in surrounding stores sometimes left their posts to watch the osprey drama that unfolded last spring. Everybody loved watching them. It was most exciting when the parents brought fish to the chicks.

One thing I learned from wildlife photography was that the closer we are to nature, the happier we are. It had always been true for me in the past, and it was certainly true for me now: I had no intention of social distancing myself from nature. Like many other people, I eagerly awaited the osprey pair, and looked forward to watching them build another nest, and photographing their next family.

In my car returning home to Boston, a fear crept into my thoughts. Was it illegal to transport toilet paper across state lines?

Kim Nagy works as a national sales manager in the natural products industry; she is also a published author and wildlife photographer. *https://www.linkedin.com/in/kimnagy/*

Our Gingerbread Cottages
by Laura Osborne

I guess I've been extremely lucky. Why, you ask. Because I've had the privilege of being in self-quarantine since February 5th. I had a freak accident, spraining my left foot and having to keep it elevated and iced. I was completely devastated.

But now I must wonder if this was, in fact, a blessing, not only in preparation for the big Coronavirus sheltering in place, but keeping me clean, healthy, and safe way before the pandemic set in. I have not had a COVID-19 test, but I am hoping that I am negative.

My foot is fine now, but the healing took six weeks, and I depended on elbow crutches all through it. I had just had cataract surgery in October and November, and I do not think that is totally healed. The year did not start off with promise.

I had plans to complete a novel and get it ready for publication. When the phone rang on January 5th, and the dental office secretary pleaded, "Laura, can you help us out this week?", I had no idea it would turn out to be more like a five-week stint, filling in as a temporary registered dental assistant, and ending on an injured foot note.

The only worry I had at that time was whether my leg would be healed and ready for walking during a Mississippi River cruise from Memphis to New Orleans my husband and I planned for our fortieth wedding anniversary. I had been looking forward to being aboard a paddlewheel riverboat for years. Then, Coronavirus had taken command of the helm and we hoped and hoped and hoped as the time went on.

"Your cruise is under consideration," the nice receptionist told us in our last communication. We found out yesterday that our cruise *has* been cancelled. A dream taken away, just like that. Boom. I guess I'm lucky that we can afford a cruise.

But the surprise of the "Coronavirus Lenten Season" came on Friday, March 13th when Cardinal Sean O'Malley of the Boston Catholic Archdiocese cancelled all masses until further notice.

The night before was when our choir usually rehearses for the Sunday mass. The choir has been a mainstay of the church for years, and I am proud to be a member.

Our director usually keeps in touch with us by email and invites us to rehearsal. He also requires that we get in touch with him in a timely fashion if we do not intend to show up. But he had just had kidney stone surgery only three days before, and I was certain he would want to rest up and heed the warnings of the latest Coronavirus threats.

I should have known better.

He has always been hard-working, wholesome, and talented, and he makes the most of the amazing organ high up in our loft that he finds more than a challenge to have repaired. He has a big job with planning the music for the masses and directing the children's choir also, and we so appreciate his leadership. He never fails to thank us for doing such a good job and making us feel like professionals. He has had this kidney condition for months, for which he had the surgery, and came to choir not even a week after. Last year, a long-time relationship of his broke up. He sometimes does not have enough music for all members, and he would probably rather not take the blame, but always apologizes, telling us, "Sorry that we're a little short, so if you could look on with your neighbor." Not that easy for a singer.

I had planned to attend the choir rehearsal of March 12th but grew tired as the day wore on into night and I decided at the very last minute to remain home. I could have forced myself to go, but, more importantly, I also had a hunch that a closing might be on the horizon for the Catholic church, on top of our director being hospitalized earlier that week.

I thought and thought because I hated to miss that choir rehearsal. I have been singing two parts, both alto and soprano, back and forth, and I was compelled to continue to be an asset. I felt guilty but I elected to text my choir director and tell him I was not able to attend the rehearsal.

Let me tell you, on March 12th, I wanted to go into lecture mode on common sense and email the following big response (late in the day prior to rehearsal):

"Mr. Maestro, thanks for conducting a rehearsal tonight, despite the many cancellations that have taken place thus far concerning the Coronavirus, but I am going to pass this evening. I am sorry for the last-minute decision, but I am truly concerned, and I believe that we are very close to a full shut-down of the Catholic Church Sunday masses. I suddenly feel very tired from my foot injury, but this is not just about me. I also want to apologize for being direct, but I feel, with the knowledge that you have been hospitalized very recently and may have been exposed to unknown bacteria, it is only natural for me to fear for not just myself, but for all the choir members coming in contact with you. You probably have not thought about this possibility, and this is by no means meant to be insinuating, hurtful, or insulting at all, but I believe it would be best if you cancelled rehearsal. I do not think we will be attending mass this Sunday, March 15th. I know I have missed a few rehearsals as of late, but I now consider this unimportant at this time. I hope everyone is staying safe and healthy and I hope to see you all soon. I pray for you and everyone and their families." Laura.

Of course, I never did even write the email. But it stayed in my head, and I woke up during the night regretting my decision not to send it, and not to attend rehearsal.

The very next day, the Cardinal made my thoughts a reality. And of course, I was amused, but frightened—that one of the biggest strongholds I had was vanished from my life.

I would give the world to have choir rehearsal.

The email prediction coincidence became a nothing deal. The Coronavirus had become the big deal. Plain and simple. Seemingly simple, but no, not simple—catastrophic. It had snuck up and had bitten our gingerbread cottage, our old, familiar maple tree, our quiet, peaceful yacht of just life. Our sacred Lenten season had been relegated to watching EWTN or viewing mass videos online.

Our faith had been assaulted, but so had the simple act of love.

On Monday, February 10th. I lost a good friend I had met at my choir over twenty years ago. She died of a brain hemorrhage. We had many lunches and coffees together. I admired her as a mentor and second mother to me. She loved to catch up on my younger person's busy life, and then I would listen to her about all her doctor appointments. Her funeral mass took place on February 14th, Valentine's Day, which turned out to be a blessing in disguise, *then*.

The following may seem unrelated, but the common thread is Valentine's Day, and, like my premonition with the church plans, it is another example of God's power and control.

My youngest sister has a birthday on this holiday and it is customary for us to go out to lunch with our other sister—three of us. But this year, I had to cancel because of the funeral. I mention this because I must confess that I had been upset with the birthday sister for her actions at an earlier function and, very unfortunately, was glad that the funeral mass had to take place that day.

What? How times change. I regret my angst, even though she, too, had injured her foot. I wondered if this was what we sometimes call a sympathy event or divine intervention, just as my injury might have been for me. It does not matter.

My sister tried to text me after the function, but I could not respond. I was reading a book that was due at the library and the deadline was fast approaching. She had found out from my other sister that I was having a difficult time getting around and that a friend of mine had passed away, but she would not give up, so as my time freed up, I gave her the opportunity to speak to me.

"I just wanted you to know that I called our aunt to explain and apologize for my behavior. She and I were both concerned about people drinking and driving. But I should not have been so outspoken and boisterous," my sister confessed to me.

"Right," I told her. "It was your decision to join Aunt Linda and me at her table. You did not have to accuse my husband of having a drinking problem when it was not the appropriate timing or setting, and when his behavior was contrary. Prior to that, you made it known that you had had a lot of drama in your household earlier with your own family pressures.

"Maybe you needed to lash out at someone else," I added about her unsavory and impolite attacks. "Let's forget it now. You know I want peace and harmony in the family."

Believe me—although this incident was a good lesson in common sense, now this all seems so insignificant in the scheme of things, and I would give the world to sit at a birthday luncheon table with my sister today.

I am fortunate to have two sisters with whom to share, to care, and to swear!!!!! Which I did when I saw all those young people on the beaches in Florida! The next day, they were closed. Good.

And now we have our stimulus package. I have food to eat, a roof over my head, and forgiveness reigns—with all the corporations for the moment forgiving their fees for everything. Let us thank God for everything, who guides us through everything.

I believe I am not alone—we would all like to have our gingerbread cottage lives back. And let's not forget the old, familiar maple tree!

Following an award-winning medical sales career, Laura Osborne, a subject of biographical and exemplary record in Who's Who?, *has published many articles, including in the national magazine,* The Advocate of the Autism Society of America, *on the importance of sibling interaction. Her feature film screenplay,* The Cross of Silvana, *based on a novel series, was a* Writer's Digest International Screenplay Competition *finalist. legacyliteraryservices.com or legacylit@verizon.net.*

Beethoven in Tirau
by Steven Sedley (New Zealand)

There was once a Beethoven festival in Tirau, formerly also known by its English name, Oxford. Perhaps the early settlers had visions of a centre of learning among the undulating fields of the South Waikato. Tirau is a small town, just a short drive from Cambridge, a picturesque little rural centre, set among some of New Zealand's most fertile farmland, at the junction of three main roads, with cafes, craft and antique shops, a gallery of corrugated iron art, a doll museum, and a museum of early New Zealand, which also houses a honey shop. You might stop there on your way to somewhere else, but it is not a place that you would expect to host a Beethoven festival. Yet, in 1947, just two years after the end of the war, Robert Pickler, a talented Hungarian violinist and Lili Kraus, a pianist famous all over Europe, performed all of Beethoven's violin and piano sonatas over three consecutive nights, June 16, 17 and 18.

People travelled long distances to come to these concerts. They spread the word that Lili Kraus was not to be missed, that such a pianist had never been heard before in New Zealand. A grand piano was freighted down from Auckland. The old Tirau Town Hall, a wooden building with good acoustics, was then still standing. There was a thunderstorm and a power cut during one of the concert; the rain drummed on the iron roof, but the two musicians coped with these difficulties, made light of them, and were loved the more for it. People would remember these concerts, the first recitals of classical music for many, for the rest of their lives.

Ed Baldwin, a young farmer, was there. He was settling back into the life he had left behind when he was shipped off to fight in North Africa and then in Italy where he took part in the closely fought North Italian campaign of the last few weeks of the war. He was mesmerised by Lili Kraus. She was a beautiful slim woman with a crown of rich dark hair. Her radiant eyes reached out to people in the audience. Ed felt that she was playing especially for him.

Lili Kraus lived in New Zealand for a year and a half after surviving internment by the Japanese in Java. Walter Nash, then the Minister of Finance, had met her in the home of the writer, H. G. Wells before the war, and like many others who got to know her, was completely enchanted. He invited her to come to New Zealand, become a New Zealander. During her time here she gave 120 concerts. She played in all the main cities, on university campuses, in schools, and in small rural towns. Every one of these recitals was for her a chance to revisit, reinterpret the music that had sustained her during her glamorous concert career in pre-war Europe and during the privations of the internment camp.

She had fled Europe and sought refuge in Java, then part of the Dutch East Indies. It was an agreeable place to shelter from the troubles in Europe. Many musicians ended up there. Then the Japanese came. They interned all Europeans. Lili Kraus was separated from her family and put in a women's prison camp. She described her experiences in her biography. She cleaned the street gutters with her bare hands. Her nails broke, her fingers split. She had to draw water from a deep well; her palms blistered. All the while she played music in her mind. When, after six months of captivity, the camp commandant recognised her name on the list of prisoners as that of the famous pianist, he found an old upright piano and asked her to play. "I just pored over the piano," she remembered, "and without any music I played on and on with my whole heart, in pain and joy." Scores of women stopped working. Others had come out of their cells to listen.

Ed, hearing Lili Kraus in Tirau, experienced something he could not put into words: a sense of illumination, understanding, transcendence. He thought of Italy, the first snowdrops sprouting from the ground after the winter storm, music emerging from silence.

It reminded him of a lonely night in a bar in Trieste. He was the last customer. The pianist, a frail young man, who looked like someone who had miraculously escaped death and was trying to put his life together again, kept playing after everyone else had left. He had closed the collection of sentimental music on his stand and dredging up music from his memory, started to play, searching for the keys that would reveal the meaning of all that he had witnessed and experienced. He played a Chopin Waltz, a simple little piece, but infused with nostalgia for a happier world. The out of tune piano added a sense of the macabre to the music. He went on to play Schumann, *The Prophet Bird*, a piece Ed himself had tried to play a long while back, then some Schubert and

Brahms, the Intermezzo based on a soulful beautiful Scottish air. Listening to the music in the gloomy bar, Ed recalled an image from the last few weeks of the war which haunted him: a German soldier hanging by one foot from the twisted girder of a demolished bridge across the river Senio, his head submerged in the swirling water. The barman started to turn off the lights. Ed went up to the pianist, put his large hand on his shoulder, hugged the emaciated young man and tears came into his eyes. His whole being was filled with an unfathomable deep sadness. Grateful that he was alive and the war was over, he was overwhelmed with longing for home, for the farm on which he grew up, the silence, the green fields, with not another human being in sight.

Ed had an old Broadwood grand piano. It came from his grandparents. A music teacher, who taught generations of country girls and boys, a small, elderly woman with hands crippled by arthritis, gave him lessons in the rudiments of music. Beyond that he taught himself. When he came back from the war he had his piano tuned and started to play again.

He lived not far from Cambridge where the viola playing principal of St. Peter's let the peaceful setting of his school be used for a summer music school. There, Lili Kraus gave master classes. Ed, though aware of his limitations as a pianist, had signed up. He listened to the other students, but when it was his turn to play he hung back. The others, young women, and a few young men, played so well, so much better than he could ever hope to. Lili Kraus noticed his diffidence, but insisted that he should take his turn. He played a little Schubert Lander. His farmer's hands looked heavy and awkward, the music sounded brittle and disjointed. Lili Kraus stroked his hand. "Relax," she said. She placed her hand on his chest. "This music is straight from the heart. It is a charming little song. Make the piano sing. Put your soul into it." And as he touched the keys, one after the other, he felt, just for an instant, that the music soared.

After hearing Lili Kraus in Tirau, he could not get her out of his head. She was so European, so different from any of the women he had ever known, with the grace and charm that embodied a rich old civilisation. He followed Lili Kraus in her travels around the world by reading every snippet of information about her that he could find. He read *Music and Musicians, The Gramophone, The Musical Times.* He cut out all the articles about her, reviews of her concerts, and pasted these in a large album. He read about the recitals she gave when she returned to Europe. She was harshly criticised. Her style was no longer in favour. After the war, people looked for something more analytical, detached, a performance with machine-like accuracy. Ed knew that these critics had missed something, the sound of hope amid the suffering that he had heard in her playing in Tirau.

He scoured music shops and bought all her gramophone records. Most of these were unavailable locally and had to be shipped from England or America. Whenever she returned to New Zealand he travelled to her concerts. Once he went back stage to meet her. He had brought along a photo of her, taken at the Cambridge Music School. The artist's room was packed with well-wishers. Ed, shy, stayed by the door. He didn't want to push himself forward. Lili caught sight of him. She turned to him and smiled.

"A beautiful concert," he mumbled.

"Why? Thank you," she said.

Did she remember him? She signed the photo and inscribed it: "With best wishes, Lili Kraus." Then she turned to one of the others in the room. "I made a bit of a mess of the last movement of the Schubert," she said and laughed in her charming, apologetic way. This is what Ed loved, Lili's humility, frailty. It was a brief memory lapse during the concert, but she had carried on and made the music sound all the more convincing. The reviews of the concert glossed over her mistakes, but stressed the sincerity and the singing quality of her playing, her ability to bring the music alive.

Back home, the old Broadwood grand was Ed's companion. In the silent isolation of his farmhouse he remembered the sound of the piano in Trieste, the insight he found in Tirau the first time he had heard Lili Kraus in concert. He thought of himself as the solitary traveller from New Zealand that Macauley, the historian, wrote about in his often quoted passage, who took his stand on a broken arch of London Bridge to sketch the ruins of St. Paul's. He was that traveller, the bridge was the bridge across the river Senio, the ruins were the devastated towns and countryside of Italy.

This passion for music he shared with no one. He was a farmer. This is how people thought of him, a capable farmer, meticulous in his attention to detail. He had a natural empathy with his animals, a feel for the land, an understanding of the seasons. His orderly dairy farm, maintained with devoted care, was run as a well-tuned business; with investments in improvements, but investments treated prudently. In his unostentatious way he prospered. He lived a quiet life, spent his money on books and gramophone records. His large library was made up of the English classics. He seldom read anything more recent than Galsworthy and Somerset Maugham except for books and journals on farming. He lived alone, but was not a recluse, always welcome in the homes of neighbours. His brother and sister had farms nearby. He was an easy guest, an educated man, interesting to talk to, and an attentive, good listener. As a boy he had been to a distinguished catholic boarding school, where the fathers shared their love of learning with him. Were it not for the war he might have gone to one of the old English universities where some of his forbearers went. He even considered, for a short while, entering the priesthood, influenced by his gentle, deep thinking, scholarly teachers.

He never married. There were women attracted to him. He was a tall, rugged, good-looking man with urbane manners that put people at ease. He was slow of speech; his words were carefully weighed and he had a slightly surprised, puzzled look of someone intently listening, eager to grasp the deeper meaning of what was said. There were women, who were his good friends and, at times, companions on social occasions, large-boned, strong, smart countrywomen, but he couldn't contemplate sharing his life and his most private moments with them. There was always something missing, things they could not talk about, experiences he could not share, memories of the war, the sense of sadness and healing, the inner peace he found in music and in his books from a different era. To women he seemed a little forbidding, too clever, all that music, and all those books, ideas too esoteric. A man like him needed to be managed, brought out of himself, encouraged to take up golf, join a club, be on committees, perhaps go into politics. And there was that photograph of Lili Kraus on his piano, a picture of a beautiful, mysterious, strange woman, out of place in that complacent rural world.

The house he lived in had been built for his grandfather, the squire, a strong-willed, restless man who cleared and worked the rich land of the

Waikato, but saw his farm as a distant frontier of an empire with its heart in old England. When Ed took over the house he changed little, but the photo of Lili Kraus on the piano gave the place a different air. She looked gentle, yet animated and sophisticated. When people asked about her, he explained:

"It is a photo of Lili Kraus, a Hungarian pianist. Few remember her now, but she was very well known in Europe in her time. She lived here just after the war. She gave many concerts; she played even here, in Tirau. People were starved for music. Those who had heard her then never forgot her." With that he would offer to play a little of one of her recordings of a Mozart Concerto.

He would offer his visitors a glass of wine, and gourmet cheese with crackers. Though not much of a drinker, Ed was a gracious host and took pride in the selection of wines he kept on hand.

"This was a pretty rough and ready place in those days," he would say. "Lili Kraus gave us a glimpse of a richer, better world."

Once Ed's nephews were old enough to help out on the farm he could go away for a few weeks. He went overseas to see opera, attend music festivals. When the time came to retire, the work on the farm became too arduous, his nephew, Burton, son of his brother, Selwyn, took over. Ed had more time for reading, playing the piano and travelling. He was the complete, self-sufficient bachelor, efficient at looking after himself. As he grew older his nephews, his nieces and their families kept their eyes on him. The warmth of his family gave him great comfort and satisfaction. When he had some dizzy spells and the occasional fall they were concerned. He knew that that the time may come when he would have to leave his spacious house and move into a retirement home. He tried to imagine living without his books and without his grand piano. "You can always get one of those electronic keyboards," one of his well-meaning neighbours said. "They don't take up much room." He shuddered at the thought.

On the day when he couldn't get out of the bath the decision was made for him. Carol, Burton's wife, found him when she called. He had run himself a bath, enjoyed soaking in the hot water, but when he tried to get out he didn't have the strength to pull himself up. The more he tried the more helpless he felt. Another of his dizzy spells. It was humiliating, Carol seeing him like this. She was very good about it, said nothing, just busied herself and got on with what she had to do. The Rosemary Randal was not bad as retirement homes go. They had talked about it before. The rooms were sunny, the staff cheerful, if somewhat patronising. He was just a helpless old man, what could he expect? Old people were treated like children. He would have to accept this; make the best of it as befitted an intelligent, thinking person.

All the things he needed to take with him were packed. Carol and Burton were there to drive him to the home. This was it; time to say farewell to all his books, writers who were his companions all his life, the hundreds of gramophone records, which no one would play anymore, and time to leave his old Broadwood grand.

Lili Kraus had died some years before in America, a muddled old lady. Her overworked fingers and joints succumbed to arthritis. In the end even her memory betrayed her, abandoned her. Her triumphs, her suffering, her single-minded determination to succeed crumbled into the helplessness of Alzheimer's disease.

Ed sat down at the piano for the last time, opened up the lid; his old man's fingers trembled as he gently stroked the opening G Major chords of Schubert's sonata. The pianissimo was barely audible. The chords had an eerie, melancholy quality. Ed played tentatively as if he had just composed the piece, brought it into being, the music coming from a deep inner source. As he played, softly, he muttered under his breath "Lili, it is my turn. I must leave too."

"It was 1947," he said, "such a long time ago. Lili Kraus came to Tirau. She gave three concerts; a great artist like her came to a little town like Tirau, and played music that people thought only belonged to the great concert halls of Europe. Our eyes, our ears, our hearts were opened. The whole world changed. We all became a little deeper, more sensitive, human beings."

With that, Ed took the scrapbook of the life of Lili Kraus from the bookshelf that filled the whole wall and put the photograph from the piano under his arm.

"Let's go," he said. "I am ready."

Born in Budapest in 1934, Steven Sedley survived the final months of the war in the Budapest ghetto. His parents each, miraculously, survived concentration camps. His father, determined to move as far away from his homeland as he

143

could to give his children a better life, moved to New Zealand in 1948. Training as a teacher, Sedley taught for some years, then ended up in educational publishing, and finally opened his own bookshop, the Horizon Bookshop, which he ran for almost 30 years. In his retirement he reads, writes, plays the violin ("not well") and is involved with the Jewish community and especially with Holocaust education.

Three Poems
by Sam Shames

Grocery Store

The tension was sharper than the deli slicer,
it was the most people I'd seen in one place in a week,
grocery shopping in the age of COVID-19.
Whole Foods on a Friday at 2 p.m.,
the packed parking lot, the stocked out shelves,
pasta, protein, parsley, and pineapples
too many & not enough,
Shoppers slowly surf through aisles,
some in gloves, some in masks,
silence fills the air while eyes sing songs of fear.
Yet hope shines in a quart of milk, a roll of paper towels, and a box of
elbow noodles.
Snaking through stacks of food, I reach the checkout.
The hero at the register scans my items,
while my face attempts to express the gratitude I cannot put into words.
Essential employees.

Family Facetimes

If laughter is the best medicine,
then family Facetimes are the new needle,
injected straight into the stomach,
belly laughs break out upon seeing your smiles,
A pandemic potion across time & space
Closing the gap in the distance between us,
socializing safely.
A respite from the fears of my own mind,
where laughter feels as distant as we're asked to be,
as if unreachable, locked away for its own good

Imprisoned & out of site,
until your faces storm the gates,
prison break,
and the giggles flash like a summer storm
The belly erupts like Vesuvius,
What's so funny?
The paradox of joy in the midst of sorrow.

River Run

River run,
for five years, the default pathway,
the unchanging asphalt
the rote route.
Today it changed.
The scenery the same,
the runners remain,
the Charles flows,
the wind blows,
but the air has changed
Clouds of uncertainty cover the sky,
invisible beneath the blue sky & yellow sun,
detectable only from the masks they wear,
the way we stare,
the space we spare,
between each other.

Sam Shames is a materials science engineer and co-founder of Embr Labs, in Cambridge, MA. https://embrlabs.com/

The Stranger
by Cami Shaskin

Author's note: This short story is nonfiction, with one exception. It indicates that the personal and worldwide events I reflect on took place <u>before</u> the opening event of the story: the walk. However, many of them actually took place a few days afterwards. In other words, for cohesiveness' sake, slight liberty has been taken in regards to timing. But the names, numbers, and stories themselves are all true.

"Have a good day, ma'am."

I was on a walk with my one-year-old son, Cody. Just him and me. I had the stroller in my hands, music from my iPhone in my ears, and the mountains in my sights. Some neighborhood kids rolled by on scooters, laughing excitedly—apparently oblivious to Earth's troubles. A grizzled, tattooed man with long hair gave a genuine smile from behind the wheel of an old truck at the corner in our neighborhood, as he waited to see if I would cross the street. I didn't need to, as home was nearby. As I rounded the corner, he said those unexpected, heartening words. "Have a good day, ma'am."

Under normal circumstances, I would have felt more wary being addressed by a man of his description. But these were far from normal circumstances. I smiled and nodded politely and we continued on our way.

The world was shutting down. Everyone knew it. The virus had already killed thousands in Italy and China. Some had reacted by stocking up on case upon case of extra toilet paper and water bottles, causing others to scratch their heads. Others poured money into masks and medicine.

Social media was having a heyday. Some users posted not-too-tasteful pictures of "backyard bidets." Others told jokes about Corona beer. Some posts were more reflective, referencing how truck drivers, grocery workers, and nurses had suddenly become much more important than NBA stars and famous entertainers.

The week prior, my church had suspended all meetings worldwide . . . indefinitely. Months in advance, before any indication of a global pandemic, church leaders had reduced the number of hours members spent in Sunday services, emphasizing a "home-centered, church-supported gospel program." Now, with this illness running rampant, we had been constrained to observe our religious practices exclusively at home. With the permission of our local bishop, families like mine were grateful to be able to hold personal church services within the walls of our own homes.

In one week, my life, along with the lives of so many others, had changed drastically. As a serious violinist, I was originally scheduled to participate in over six performances and nine rehearsals in the month of March alone. The music and ensembles were quite varied. I had already performed in a concert for the American Choral Directors Association during the first weekend of the month. For upcoming performances in March, there was everything from Latter-day Saint hymn arrangements— as part of a weekly television broadcast of Music and the Spoken Word with the Tabernacle Choir at Temple Square, to works by Mozart, Beethoven, and Brahms with the American West Symphony, to a solo rendition of Sibelius' famous theme from Finlandia for a Spring Women's Conference. I was even slated to conduct the local Youth Symphony performing Grieg's Holberg Suite. And yet, government leaders were recommending no gatherings of over a hundred people. Then twenty people. Then ten. With new precautions added every day, all of my concerts were quickly—almost magically—canceled! I also soon determined that I would need to change the violin lessons I taught on a weekly basis to virtual lessons, hoping that parents would be willing to try the experiment (without getting too used to it).

Going out to dinner had recently proved eye-opening. I was at a restaurant with my husband when it was already common knowledge that the symptoms of COVID-19 were fever, a dry cough, and shortness of breath. Unfortunately, during dinner, I swallowed wrong and some air went down the wrong tube. As I began to cough in response, all conversation around us at the diner ceased, and I suddenly felt the eyes of all around me staring, as if to say, "How could you think to come out in public?!"

A few days later, I went to Cafe Rio with my aunt, days prior to a ban on dine-in eating. As if the workers knew what was coming, they automatically put all orders, including ours, into to-go bags, though we told them we hadn't planned on taking our food out. The cashier, though cordial, was also insistent. "No, we have to do this." My aunt predicted correctly that this was likely the last time we'd be able to go out to eat for a long time.

Amid the uncertainty and tumult which had become commonplace, I also had a birthday. I had purchased a plane ticket to visit my brother in Colorado as a birthday present to myself. Hours before I was to leave, the White House held a news conference in which all Americans were cautioned to cancel "all discretionary travel." I canceled my plane ticket.

And I wasn't the only one making adjustments. My friend Kelly, a school teacher, posted a picture showing fellow teachers handing assignments out the windows of schools to teenagers standing on tip-toe to reach their assigned Chromebook. Parents struggled to suddenly homeschool their children. A buzz of anxiety met suddenly desperate shoppers. (In fact, the only true concern I had felt recently was in the crowded grocery store, surrounded by other worried customers. They were patient, but guarded. Many, like me, were witnessing empty shelves for the first time.)

Would this pandemic change our society forever? And how? Would virtual *everything* become the new norm? Would fast food workers be

149

replaced by robots in the future? After all, a robot wouldn't be contagious and wouldn't be reliant on a steady income in troubled times.

They say when it rains, it pours. I live in Utah. On March 18, a 5.7 magnitude earthquake in Magna jolted my husband and me from our sleep. Utahns across the region had a similar experience. Aftershocks continued throughout the day and week. The airport shut down, and warnings were being sent to cellphones to avoid all travel into the Salt Lake Valley as crews assessed the damage. One of my acquaintances on Facebook vented about how a full moon, Friday the 13th, a global pandemic, and now an earthquake had all happened in the same week. She quipped, "You can't make this stuff up!" And it was true. Apparently Someone had His methods and reasons . . .

And yet, through all the chaos, here was a stranger wishing me a good day! Could it be that tough times in America reveal the tough goodness of people in our communities? People everywhere smiling and saying, "It's okay," when they're bumped into in the store entrance . . . Local musicians, many of them my friends, volunteering to play their instruments live on the internet to a skyrocketing population of instant shut-ins . . . Famous institutions offering free opera, free software, free animal shows, all accessible from the comfort of your living room.

Amid "social distancing" came an almost telepathic closeness between family, neighbors, and friends. Suddenly long lost relatives were inquiring through the internet if I was okay. One violin student on vacation across the country, where deaths from the virus were high, texted me to find out if I had suffered any damage from the earthquake. My mom even checked with me to see if I had enough toilet paper.

Yes, this is a time of bewilderment and anxiety. Drastic changes have become expected. Regulations continue to tighten regularly. But for me, this is also a time of peace and hope, as I reflect, not on the selfishness of hoarders or the crassness of bored internet users, but on one random stranger who took the time to say, "Have a good day, ma'am."

Cami Shaskin is a Utah native, homemaker and violin teacher, with a graduate degree in Music Education from UNC (Greeley) and a B.A. and minor in Language and Computers from Brigham Young University.

A View from the Other End

Flushed with Pride
or, On a Roll
by Gerald Elias in Salt Lake City.
Assisted by
my daughter, Kate Elias, and her husband, Brick Maier, in Seattle.

Is this what it takes? Why is it that it's only when times are tough, in these dark days, when you appreciate me? That's when you realize how much you need me. Not yesterday. Not tomorrow. Only today. Finally.

And you expect my gratitude? When was the last time you didn't take me for granted? When you didn't make sophomoric jokes about me to your friends?

And yet. And yet. When you reach out, I'm there for you. Always. And you know that. I'm there for you. Again. And again. And again. Even though both you and I know you'll strip layer after layer off me, until there's nothing left of me except a hollow cylinder that you discard into the trash without a second thought.

We share the most intimate spaces. I see a part of you no one else does. Or very few. Sometimes you want me to be soft. Other times strong. Even ultra-strong. That costs extra. You know that. Does that make you chafe? That's for you to decide.

Six equals eight. Eight equals twelve. Twelve equals...infinity. It never ends.

Or does it?

And when I'm not there, when you've used me all up, what do you do? Who do you turn to? A little squirt?

Maybe you've considered the new Poseidon's Rocket, with "aqua piston technology." This newfangled gadget, with so many buttons and levers, won't last. Sure, it comes with "Hades breath vents" for "lightly

152

warmed buns," but what happens when it doesn't turn on? I, on the other hand, just keep on rolling along. I've got you covered.

So finally, in these dark times, I've gained your attention. You fight over me. I am George Clooney. I am the Dalai Lama. I occupy a hallowed place next to your porcelain shrine. (And yet, I fear this time of adulation will, by necessity, be skidding to a halt. We in the business have long maintained the popular illusion that I am the best—the *only*—option. But even as I become more valuable, the truth that much of the world has known for so long may soon be dawning on this society: that a dry, wadded scrap of paper may not, after all, be the ideal choice for the job at hand.)

But still, you use me. And after you use me, you're feeling so much better, while I'm totally wiped and things inevitably spiral down. You go on your merry way.

They say a dog is man's best friend. But when push comes to shove, who do you really need by your side?

We're all in this together. We'll get through it. Be well. Be safe. Smile.

Acknowledgements

First of all, a great big thankyou to all the authors of all stripes who joyfully gave of themselves to contribute their stories for no compensation whatsoever. Each story required a continuous stream of back-and-forth emails, around the country and around the globe. That it all came together so quickly is a tribute to their sticktoitiveness and pride in doing something to the best of their abilities and for a good cause.

I'd also like to give a shout-out to my dear friend, Sergio Pallottelli, for helping translate *Lettere* on the spur of the moment and in between nonstop video lessons with his many flute students. For the same story, I'd like to thank my daughter, Kate, for doing the formatting of the Italian version of the letters. She had a vested interest, I suppose: Johanna Fridrich and Kate have been friends since we lived in Umbria in 1997. And finally, a big hug for my wife, Cecily, who not only took care of the house and chores while I chugged along with this, she was also my literary adviser and expert proofreader.

If you enjoyed this book, *please* encourage your friends and family to pick up a copy. But whether you did or not, here's the simple way you can donate to the Red Cross: redcross.org/donate

Thank you.

Made in the USA
San Bernardino, CA
15 April 2020

67804178R00100